ONE-THIRD NERD

ONE-THIRD NERD

GENNIFER CHOLDENKO

ILLUSTRATED BY
ÉGLANTINE CEULEMANS

A Yearling Book

Text copyright © 2019 by Gennifer Choldenko
Cover art and interior illustrations copyright © 2019 by Églantine Ceulemans

All rights reserved. Published in the United States by Yearling, an imprint of
Random House Children's Books, a division of Penguin Random House LLC,
New York. Originally published in hardcover in the United States by
Wendy Lamb Books, an imprint of Random House Children's Books,
a division of Penguin Random House LLC, New York, in 2019.

Visit us on the Web! rhcbooks.com

Educators and librarians, for a variety of teaching tools, visit us at
RHTeachersLibrarians.com

The Library of Congress has cataloged
the hardcover edition of this work as follows:
Names: Choldenko, Gennifer, author. | Ceulemans, Eglantine, illustrator.
Title: One-third nerd / by Gennifer Choldenko ; illustrations by Eglantine
Ceulemans. Description: First edition. | New York : Wendy Lamb Books, an
imprint of Random House Children's Books, [2019] | Summary: Ten-year-old
Liam and his two younger sisters, precocious third-grader Dakota and second-
grader Izzy, who has Down syndrome, face the possibility of losing their
beloved dog, Cupcake, who keeps urinating on their apartment's carpet. |
Identifiers: LCCN 2018005488 (print) | LCCN 2018013437 (ebook) |
ISBN 978-1-5247-1890-9 (ebook) | ISBN 978-1-5247-1888-6 (trade) |
ISBN 978-1-5247-1889-3 (lib. bdg.)
Subjects: | CYAC: Brothers and sisters—Fiction. | Family life—Fiction. |
German shepherd dog—Fiction. | Dogs—Fiction. | Down syndrome—Fiction. |
People with mental disabilities—Fiction. | Apartment houses—Fiction.
Classification: LCC PZ7.C446265 (ebook) |
LCC PZ7.C446265 One 2019 (print) | DDC [Fic]—dc23

ISBN 978-1-5247-1891-6 (pbk.)

Printed in the United States of America
10 9 8 7 6 5 4 3 2 1
First Yearling Edition 2020

Random House Children's Books supports the First Amendment
and celebrates the right to read.

To Elizabeth Harding,
who always has my back

CONTENTS

ONE-THIRD NERD

1

PEE IN THE FRIDGE

Fifth grade is not for amateurs.

You have to watch yourself. Kids notice stuff.

What books you read. What sports you follow. What devices you own. And how nerdy you are.

A little nerdy is good; you can fix the game controller. But if you're the kid who gets the teacher's website up and running so everyone has more homework . . . that's too nerdy.

And then there are the subtle things, like how you raise your hand. Should you raise it high and eager? Low and mouselike? Rotate your palm? Flap it all around? Or does your arm come up straight and slow like a log on a pulley?

Same with turning your homework in. Do you put it on the top of the pile? Or the bottom? Do you fold it like a paper airplane and fly it to your teacher's desk? Deliver it by drone? Or do you send it up the classroom aisle in the mouth of a robotic device?

I could probably manage all this okay if it weren't for my sisters.

Dakota, the third grader, is the worst.

I finally get up the courage to talk to the girl everyone thinks is cute and Dakota shouts across the playground, "Liam, I need toilet paper from the boys' bathroom. There's none in the girls'."

Izzy, the second grader, is a hugger. The custodian, the crossing guard, my coach . . . Izzy hugs everyone.

Unfortunately, my sisters and I look alike: blond hair, blue eyes, and on the short side, so I can't hide the fact that I'm their brother.

Then there's our dog, Cupcake, a black and tan German shepherd with crooked front teeth and shiny black lips. Cupcake has little accidents in our apartment.

Did I mention we live under the landlord?

Not that poor pee control would be a good idea in any house, but it's especially bad when you live close to your landlord.

Other problems? Cupcake howls when the microwave dings. And Izzy sings all the time.

Luckily, the landlord, Mr. Torpse, is hard of hearing. Once he takes his hearing aids out, Izzy can sing as much as she wants. How do we know they're out? He turns his TV up so loud it's like the voice of our principal booming from the PA at school.

We hear every sound Torpse makes. When he belches, shouts at the radio, or goes to the toilet. Plus, he spies on us. He says he only comes downstairs to water the plants, right outside his window, but since there's nothing to water but dried-up weeds, I wonder.

So I don't bring friends to our apartment. I don't tell people where I live. I don't even write my address on the forms at school.

The only person who knows the truth is my best friend, Dodge, and he won't tell anyone.

Dodge comes over every day. His grandpa Crash watches us if my mom has to work late. Some days, Crash can't get out of work either, and then I'm the one in charge for a little while.

I don't see Crash's car, so I'm guessing today will be one of those days.

Dodge, Dakota, and I walk from the bus stop. We climb down the steep stairs to our apartment, careful to avoid the rotted wood steps that sink when you step on them. I pull the blue key with the smiley-face sticker out from under my shirt, where it hangs on a string, and I unlock the door.

Inside, I open the patio slider to let Cupcake in. She is crazy excited to see me, jumping all around.

I follow Dodge to the tiny kitchen. Dodge finds the crackers and he's about to wash them down with lemonade. He squints at the glass. "Did your mom buy a new brand?"

I catch a whiff and then snatch his glass out of his hand. It smells like pee!

· 4 ·

"Sorry, um . . ." I run to the bathroom, dump it, and hurry back to pour him some actual lemonade in a new glass.

Who would put a glass of pee in the fridge?

Dakota!

Dakota has been working on the problem of why Cupcake has lost pee control.

She never had a problem until a few months ago. We housebroke her when she was little.

She learned so quickly. What a smart, cute puppy she was. She had the softest fur, floppy ears, and giant paws, and she made funny groaning sounds—like a dog's version of a purr. The week after my parents split up, Mom got us Cupcake. The first night we had her, she chewed off the top of a Tupperware container and wolfed down the cupcakes inside. That's how she got her name.

When we lived in our old house, there was a yard for Cupcake. But in January Mom and Dad sold our house and we rented this place. Now the "yard" is a tiny patio with one plant trying hard to grow out of a crack in the cement. When it produces a leaf, Cupcake pees on it and it flops over again.

My job is walking Cupcake. Mom won't let Dakota or Izzy walk her because it isn't safe in our neighborhood, but I never worry. Cupcake is the world's best watchdog. Once, a bodybuilder in a camouflage vest walked too close to me and Cupcake growled. Now when that guy sees me, he runs to the other side of the street.

I never feel short when I walk Cupcake. Though I do wish we'd named her something more ferocious, like Dude or Brute.

"Look, um, I'm sorry about the lemonade," I mumble to Dodge when we're out on the street.

Dodge shrugs. That's Dodge for you. He rolls with everything.

We take turns on the skateboard hanging on to Cupcake's harness so she'll haul us up the hill; then we start talking about what happened in class.

"Can you believe Moses got in Leadership already? He's been here . . . what . . . three weeks?" I say.

Leadership is kind of like Student Council, only the teachers choose who will be on it. I like it. It makes me feel important. Dodge was in Leadership, but he doesn't want to have to talk that much, so he got out.

"Moses is nice," Dodge says.

I throw the tennis ball for Cupcake, then jump back on my board. "Have you seen him play? He's got a killer serve, and his overhead smash bounces over the fence."

Dodge nods. "I heard he's on two tennis teams—ours, and another at some club."

"A club . . . ? He's rich too?" I sigh. "One-third nerd, one-third athlete, one-third rich kid. Moses has it all."

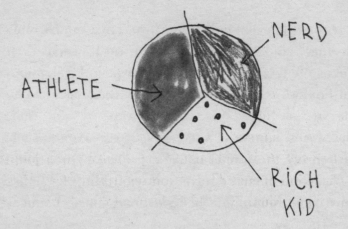

"Like what's-his-name, the guy who started Facebook?"

"Mark Zuckerberg?"

"Yeah, him. Super nerd. Genius. Is he good at sports?"

"Has to be," I say. "There are sports everywhere on Facebook. So, who would you rather be: Mark Zuckerberg or Roger Federer?"

Roger Federer is the world's best tennis player. We love him because he always wins without ever sweating or grunting or yanking at his underwear. I have a life-size cardboard Roger Federer in my room. Every month I measure my height against his. Just twenty-two inches to go.

"Federer, duh," Dodge says.

I roll the board to Dodge. "Do you think Moses is better than Roger was when he was our age?"

Dodge shrugs. Dodge and I are both on the tennis team. Dodge likes to play, but not as much as I do.

I don't ask him what I really want to know: Am I as good as Roger was when he was my age? And what would happen if I played Moses? Would I get crushed or . . . would he?

This kind of stuff doesn't matter to Dodge. I don't know why it matters so much to me.

2

TORPSE THE CORPSE

When we get back from walking Cupcake, Dakota has her head in the refrigerator. "Who messed with yesterday's sample?" she shouts.

"Why'd you put that in the fridge? Dodge almost drank it," I whisper.

"Do you want to spend the rest of your life cleaning up dog pee?" Dakota wants to know.

"No. But, Dakota, that's gross. Besides, don't you have to have a healthy sample? To compare, you know, with what's in her pee now?" I ask.

"I have one."

"You took a sample before she got sick?"

Dakota leans in. "I have samples *from everyone.*"

This is the problem with asking Dakota questions. You really don't want to hear the answers.

"Why?" I ask.

"You have to have a baseline," she explains.

"But how would you know to get a baseline?"

"I read, Liam. Don't you read?"

I close the refrigerator carefully, because otherwise the door comes off the hinges and squashes your toe. "How did you collect them?"

"We're not supposed to flush every time. If it's yellow, leave it mellow. If it's brown, flush it down."

"Ew." I make a face. "Where do you keep the samples?"

"You saw where I keep them: the refrigerator."

"But Mom cleans it out every week." I make a pouch with my shirt and load in kale chips. They taste like deep-fried tea bags, but Mom says kale will help me grow.

Dakota grins. "I take them out when we bring the grocery bags in and put them back after she's unloaded everything."

"Jeez, Dakota, get a life, will you?"

Dodge and I head for my room.

She chases after us. "If you're going to be a scientist, you have to work hard. That's what Mom says. Can I play?"

"No." I keep walking.

She dives in front of me. "There's something important I have to say."

I roll my eyes.

"Lawrence Hall of Science has job openings. I saw on their website. I could make adult-size money."

"They aren't looking for eight-year-olds who only have time at recess."

"You can't refuse to hire someone because of their age. That's age re-crim-ination, Crash said. I applied already, but they haven't gotten back to me yet."

"I'll bet," I say.

"Liam, look!" She points out the window to the low gray clouds. "El Niño is coming. We can't leave Cupcake out in the rain, and if we bring her in, she'll pee on the rugs."

Dakota's right. "You figured out anything with your stupid samples?"

She shakes her head. "I may need to consult a veterinarian."

We took Cupcake to the vet a few months ago because she had an even grosser problem: diarrhea.

We got medicine for it, which worked. But the visit cost $331, with the tests and the medicine and everything. And then she started to pee a lot. Mom called the vet, who said we needed to take Cupcake to the veterinary school at UC Davis for further study, because she didn't know what the problem was. Mom asked her how much

UC Davis would cost. The vet said, "Three thousand dollars. Maybe."

"We could ask Dad," Dakota suggests.

My father lives across town. He'll be by today, because on Tuesdays he brings over dinner in a Pyrex dish and leaves it on the doorstep. It will be something yummy, like barbeque ribs or homemade macaroni and cheese. My dad's mac and cheese is so good that Dakota mailed some to the President.

She never heard back from the White House, though. Big surprise.

Dad doesn't come until five, but today Dakota goes out early to wait for him. She finishes her homework and then does extra work. Her teacher, Mrs. Johnson, doesn't give assignments for extra credit, so she has to make up her own. It's pretty sad.

Mom doesn't like us hanging around outside, but there's no telling Dakota that. She's too young to understand what you're supposed to be afraid of. Besides, she's got Cupcake with her.

In my room, I close the door and Dodge and I take turns with the game controller. That's the one good thing about being the only boy in an apartment full of girls. I get my own room. Izzy and Dakota have to share.

My room is tan and blue and has posters of Star Wars and Bigfoot, plus a life-size cardboard Roger

Federer that Izzy and Dakota are forbidden to ever touch.

Mom sleeps in the living room, since she goes to bed later than everyone else.

Just as Dodge gets to level 25, we hear the explosion.

Cupcake barks. I run outside.

"Did you hear that?" Dakota asks, her voice thick, her hands covered with watermelon. She taps her phone, which used to be my phone. "The website said the exploding watermelon experiment is hard to do. I did it and I got it on video." She grins.

"We heard. Everybody in the whole state heard, including Torpse without his hearing aids." I survey the mess. Pieces of red watermelon flesh slop down the windows and hang from the stairs; juice puddles on the doormat.

"Torpse isn't home. Today is his yoga class, I think."

I get the mop and hand it to her. You wouldn't believe what a mess an exploding watermelon makes. "See," Dakota says, "you put all these thick rubber bands around the center and that causes some kind of pressure that makes it explode."

"I hope you're right about Torpse," I say.

Mom said we're not supposed to call him Torpse the Corpse because then Izzy starts up with it. Last week she said, "Hello, Mr. Torpse the Corpse." And then she hugged him. Luckily, Izzy doesn't speak clearly, so Torpse didn't catch what she said.

"I'm always right," Dakota says as she clicks on the explosion video. Cupcake curls up at Dakota's feet as Dodge and I lean in to watch.

"Wow," Dodge says. "Play it again."

Just as Dakota pushes play, there are footsteps up above.

"Daddy!" Dakota grabs the phone and starts up the stairs. "Oh." Her voice gets funny, like she swallowed a balloon's worth of helium.

"Uh-oh, Torpse!" I whisper.

But when the man comes down the stairs, he isn't Torpse.

He's a policeman.

3

I THOUGHT THIS ONLY
HAPPENED TO TEENAGERS

A short policeman with a bushy mustache comes down the stairs, followed by a tall policewoman. Both have thick black belts weighed down with guns.

Guns!

Dakota always gets us in trouble, but never with the police! Don't you have to be at least twelve for that?

Cupcake is barking. "Shush," I say. My arms tremble as I shove her inside.

"Where are your parents?" the lady cop asks.

"Our mom isn't home yet. She's taking our little sister, Izzy, to speech therapy. Our dad doesn't live here."

"But he's going to drop by with beef Wellington," Dakota chimes in.

"Beef Wellington, is it?" The policewoman eyes her partner. "So, you three live here?" She nods toward our basement apartment.

"Dakota and I do." I can't take my eyes off their guns. "Dodge lives on Barnett."

"Dodge?" The lady cop squints at Dodge, who is looking a little green.

"His real name is Sebastian Dodge, but nobody calls him that," I explain.

"Can you speak, Dodge?" the policewoman asks.

"Yes, ma'am," he mutters.

"So, what happened here? We got a report there was a loud noise, like an explosion."

"Yes, ma'am," I say. "But it wasn't a real explosion."

"It was too a *real* explosion." Dakota glares at me. She's hopping around all excited like she thinks

the cops are giving out extra credit. For a smart girl, she sure can be stupid. I step on her toe to shut her up.

It doesn't work.

"Do you want to see?" Dakota asks, offering up the phone.

The lady cop raises one eyebrow. Now her eyes seem to be operating independently. Neither of them likes us.

"Everybody at school is going to love this," Dakota whispers to her.

"Are you using explosives?" the policewoman asks.

"No! Oh, no . . . It's a science experiment!" I explain.

The policewoman's finger beckons. "Let's have a look."

Dakota smiles like she's going to be a YouTube star. She starts the video on my old phone. It's a junky little phone, but Dakota did a good job filming.

The lady cop stares down at her. "They taught you this at school?"

"Not exactly," Dakota admits.

"How'd you learn it?"

"Online," Dakota tells her.

"So you're researching explosive devices?"

Dakota nods.

The policewoman is taking notes the old way: with paper and pencil. "Did an adult put you up to this?" she asks.

I step forward. "No! It isn't like that. She's only trying for extra credit. She'll do anything for extra credit."

"Extra credit." The cops look at each other.

"Look, you can't be doing this in the stairwell of your building, scaring the neighbors." The policewoman drops Dakota's cell in a plastic bag and hands the bag to the policeman, who holds it delicately between two fingers.

"Hey, that's mine!" Dakota says as the stairwell vibrates with footsteps. Dad's feet appear, then Dad's legs, and then Dad, wearing his usual dad outfit. Khaki shorts. White shirt. Flip-flops.

"Well, hello," Dad says, and then he sees the police, and he makes a sound like Cupcake when you step on her paw.

The policewoman points at the bag Dad is holding. "Beef Wellington."

My father nods. "What is going on?" He mouths the question to me.

"Your name, sir?" the policewoman asks.

"Will Rose."

"These are your children, Mr. Rose?"

"Liam and Dakota. Not Dodge."

"Your kids have been using explosive materials in the stairwell, disturbing the neighbors. They claim it's a science experiment."

"It *is* a science experiment," Dakota insists.

"It seems to me the real problem is a lack of supervision," the policewoman continues.

"Usually Crash, Dodge's grandfather, watches them." Dad frowns at Dodge. "Where is he today?"

"He had to work late at the police station. He'll be here any minute," Dodge mumbles.

"The station?" The lady cop's eyebrows rise.

"He's a detective," Dodge says. "Jimmy Hernandez."

The policewoman nods. "How old are these children, Mr. Rose?"

"Liam and Dodge are ten. Dakota is eight," Dad says.

"Young to be left alone, especially here." She looks over to the side yard, where the abandoned washing machine sits.

"I'll talk to my ex-wife about it."

"You do that, Mr. Rose," the lady cop says as the radio on the policeman's shoulder begins to crackle. He picks it up and listens. Then he catches his partner's eye and motions with his head toward the stairs.

"Now, you listen." The lady cop points at Dakota. "You are not to do your science experiments unless an adult is present. We're not going to be nearly so lenient if we're called out here again. You understand, young lady?"

"Yes, ma'am." Dakota puffs up her chest. "May I have my phone back? It's only kinda mine. I won it off a bet with Liam."

"Dakota." Dad puts his finger to his mouth. "If a police officer wants to keep your phone, that is her prerogative."

"I don't think she understands the gravity of the situation," the policewoman tells Dad.

"I do so. I did a report on gravity. Ask me anything. *I know!*" Dakota blurts out.

"Dakota, shhh!" Dad says.

Dakota's teeth clack shut.

The policeman hands the plastic bag back. His eyes fix on Dad. "Should we be called back here again, we'll need to take serious action."

"I understand," Dad says.

"I hope you can impress that fact on your offspring."

Dad's face turns pink.

"All right, then." The police officers start up the stairs. "Enjoy your beef Wellington, Mr. Rose."

"He's not going to have any," Dakota calls after them. "He just brings it for us."

"Dakota," Dad says

"Well, you're not, are you?" she asks.

Dad groans.

I can't believe the police came. I thought that only happened to teenagers. "Sorry, Dad," I say.

Dakota doesn't apologize. She's allergic to the words "I'm sorry." Her bottom lip puffs out. "But, Dad, don't you see? My teacher said she couldn't get this to work and I did *first time!*"

"That's good, honey, but . . ."

Dakota's lip trembles. "I'm going to be a scientist or be Bill Gates, just like you said."

Dad sighs. His voice is gentle. "Remember when we talked about self-control?"

"Your self is the driver and your body is the car," Dakota says. "The driver has to control the car, which includes the car's mouth, even though cars don't have mouths."

"Right," Dad says.

Dakota holds her hand over her mouth to keep herself from talking. Then she spreads her fingers and mumbles, "I'm supposed to keep quiet until I'm old and my teeth fall out and I have to buy pretend ones, which Crash says do not work very well. He says if young people needed new teeth, then someone would make sure they worked better."

"Dakota, sweetie, that's not what I said," Dad says.

Dakota looks like a beach ball with the air leaked out. She drags herself in the front door.

My father stares after her, shaking his head. "What are we going to do about her?" he asks Dodge and me.

I like the way he asks us grown-up questions.

"She gets excited about stuff and then she can't stop," I explain.

"That what you think, Dodge?" my father asks.

Dodge nods. "She's nice, though," he mumbles, and then turns red.

My father smiles. "That may be more than I've ever heard you say, Dodge."

Dodge's face gets even redder. He talks to Dakota and Izzy and me, but not that much to anyone else.

Dad folds his big body down on the stairs. Dad is tall. I'm planning to be tall just like him.

He doesn't go inside our place, though. Mom doesn't go into his apartment and he doesn't go into hers.

Before they got divorced, they spent a lot of time cooking together. I used to have to do taste tests about whose spaghetti sauce was better. Dad would pout if I didn't say his. Christmas was the best. When we woke up Christmas morning, they were both there. Dad made cinnamon rolls. Mom made hash browns and scrambled eggs and then snags, which is Australian for sausages. Mom grew up in Australia, where they go to the beach on Christmas, so that's what we always do.

Dad looks from me to Dodge and back again. "How's your tennis game these days?"

"Good." I smile. I'm okay at most sports, but put a tennis racket in my hand and it's like when Ollivander hands Harry Potter his wand. Even back in first grade when Crash showed us how to hit with our thrift store rackets, it was like that. That was when we used these special balls—with red spots— that didn't bounce very high.

"Let me know when you have a match."

I nod.

"And you ought to apologize to the neighbors when your mom gets home," Dad tells me.

"Why me? It was Dakota who did it."

"At least go with her, all right? She needs you more than you know."

I groan. "Do you know how embarrassing she is?"

"Yes," he says. "I do. And I also know you're a terrific big brother."

Dad pulls out his phone and brings up the traffic, then shakes his head. "I got to get going. I'm sorry, no insurance lesson today."

I try to look disappointed. Dad has a new job as an insurance agent. Insurance is where you pay a little money every month so the company will pay you a pile of money if something bad happens. I'd rather chew cement than hear about insurance, but I don't want to hurt Dad's feelings.

"Don't nuke the beef Wellington or it gets tough. I packed a little berry compote for dessert. It's good with vanilla ice cream. Tell me what your mother says."

He can't wait to hear what Mom thinks about his food.

"Wait!" Dakota sticks her head out the front door. She must have been listening at the window, which is rusted permanently open. "We need money to take Cupcake to the vet."

Dad stands up, brushes his shorts off, and digs his wallet out of his back pocket. "Twenty bucks do?"

She smushes her face against the screen. "No."

"How much, then?" he asks.

"Three thousand dollars," Dakota says.

Dad snorts. "Look, sweetie, I know you love that dog. My screen saver is a picture of you three and that puppy dressed in matching pajamas. But money is tight right now and the dog was your mother's idea." He's halfway up the stairs. "Don't forget to give Izzy a hug from me. And tell your mom I can take Izzy to speech therapy on Thursday," he calls back.

"How about kitty litter?" Dakota calls after him.

"Kitty litter?" I ask.

She nods. "We can teach Cupcake to pee in a box like a cat."

I roll my eyes.

"Wait! Wait! We'll take the twenty," Dakota shouts, but Dad is flip-flopping back to his car, too far away already.

Dakota opens our apartment door and swings it back and forth. *Squeak-squareek. Squeak-squareek.* "With his twenty, we'd only need two thousand nine hundred and eighty dollars," she says. But she doesn't run after him and neither do I.

4

SUPERPOWERS I DON'T HAVE

Dodge is chewing paper when Mom and Izzy get home. He wads it up and sprinkles it with sugar. It's not so bad, actually. I tried it.

Cupcake waits for the sugar to slide onto the floor and then she licks it up.

Mom kisses us, then calls Crash to tell him she's home so he doesn't have to come over. She sticks the beef Wellington in the oven before she takes her purse off her shoulder. Cupcake curls around Mom's and Izzy's legs. Mom is always happy to see us. But Cupcake goes practically psychotic whenever one of us comes home.

Izzy gives Cupcake a kiss on her wet black nose. Then she hugs me, Dakota, and Dodge.

My mom has a long blond ponytail that swings when she walks. She likes puzzles and kangaroos and things from Australia. She uses weird words sometimes. Like the toilet is "the dunny," and lottery tickets are "scratchies." She is the assistant manager at Fiorelli's Restaurant.

Dodge and I set the table. Dodge likes eating with us because Crash cooks weird food, like chocolate cake with beets in it, and popcorn with ketchup. Dodge is always trying to convince him to make his grandma Lily's pot roast or tamales or chimichangas or chocolate chip Rice Krispies cookies. But Dodge's grandma Lily died a few years ago and Crash doesn't want to cook from her recipes. Dodge doesn't know why.

I wait until we're done with dessert to suggest to Mom that maybe she should call Dad.

"Why?" she asks.

Dakota slides off her chair.

Mom digs a tunnel in her ice cream. "Izzy's speech therapist was late. What happened?"

Dodge looks at me. I clear my throat. "The police came. Dakota tried out a new experiment. It was loud."

Mom puts down her spoon. "Mr. Torpse?" she whispers.

"He wasn't home. Somebody else must have called."

"Somebody else?" She holds her head like it hurts. "I don't know if that's good news or bad."

"Good news. The police are good." Izzy wipes her mouth. "I'm using napkin. And Purpley is using napkin too." Izzy wipes the purple horse's mouth, then puts him in her lap.

"Good job." Mom nods.

Izzy's smile shines.

Mom peeks under the table at Dakota. "Why didn't you wait until I came home to do the experiment?"

Dakota sighs. "I wanted to see if I could do it."

"What about that promise you made after the Mentos explosion?"

"Oh. Yeah," Dakota says.

Mom looks at me. "What did the police say?"

"That we shouldn't be left alone."

"And that's what your father wants to talk to me about?"

I nod.

My mother sighs. She carries her bowl into the kitchen and turns on the faucet full force. The leftover ice cream splashes out. "Better start emailing your apologies, Dakota. One to your father. One to the neighbors. I'll track down the email addresses."

The police come and that's all the punishment Dakota gets!

Girls get off way easier than guys do. I'm happy Dakota is emailing, though. Then I won't have to go with her to deliver her apologies.

Dakota crawls out from under the table. We exchange a look. Even she knows this isn't a bad punishment. Mom must be in a good mood. Probably she got all the words in the *New York Times* crossword this morning.

Mom helps Izzy do her homework. Izzy can read okay, if the books don't have many words in them.

When Dakota finishes her emails, she shows them to Dodge and me.

Hello, Parental Unit.

I am sorry about the police. Mom says I need to work on my before thinking. Before I do stuff I'm supposed to think. It's hard to keep your brain thinking in the right direction every minute. Maybe there should be traffic lights up there.

Bye,

☺ Dakota ☺

Hello, Neighbors.

I am sorry if I disturbed any one of the 1,440 minutes in your day. I will do only quiet explosions from now on. But I don't know how you make mittens or Kleenex explode.

From,

☺ Dakota ☺

Mom is helping Izzy practice her writing when Dakota brings our old laptop to her. Mom reads the emails and then asks: "Do you mean that?"

"Sort of," Dakota says.

Mom sighs. "I suppose that's a start. Go ahead and send the one to Dad. The neighbors' email needs work."

"Like what?"

"The part about the quiet explosions."

Dakota's arms are crossed. "How am I supposed to win a Nobel Prize, then?"

Mom rolls her eyes.

It's getting late, so we walk Dodge home. Mom and Cupcake come along because we aren't allowed to go places by ourselves in the dark. Izzy holds Dodge's hand, which would be humiliating if it were anyone besides Dodge.

Dodge lives up near the freeway in a small house with a tiny porch full of his grandma's flowers. Crash makes sure every one of her plants stays alive. He says there should be a 911 for plant emergencies.

Dodge waves goodbye and opens the front door. Dodge's house is crowded. The table is buried under a mound of junk mail. There are newspapers stacked all around, and Book of the Month Club packages. Crash won't throw anything away that has Lily's name on it.

On the way home, Mom stops to talk to the neighbor with all the plants on her patio. I can't imagine who complained, because our neighbors are nice; it's only the landlord who isn't.

We run on ahead with Cupcake, who is panting hard because a truck just passed by. Cupcake thinks it's her job to bark at trucks.

"We need to figure out a way to make some money for the vet," Dakota announces.

"Money in Mom's purse," Izzy says.

"But that's her money," I say, pine needles crackling under my feet. "We need our money."

"Money in the bank," Izzy says.

"That's the bank's money."

Izzy shakes her head. "The bank gives Mom money."

"That's her money that the bank is borrowing," Dakota says.

I shake my head at Dakota. "Don't get all technical on Izzy," I whisper.

Cupcake waits patiently for us to kick a pinecone, then dashes after it, jerking the leash.

"The bank keeps Mom's money in a safe place. When we get home, we'll get the Monopoly game money out," I tell Izzy.

"Money!" Izzy skips after Cupcake.

"What if we did experiments in the park?" Dakota suggests. "We could pass a hat for money. We could do the watermelon explosion."

"Too loud and messy. Somebody will call the police."

"How about the Mentos explosion?"

"Everybody knows that one. Nobody would pay to see it." I breathe in the smell of someone's barbeque. "Besides, we'd have to buy the Diet Coke and the Mentos."

"Mom will buy them," Dakota says.

"Not after last time." A few weeks ago, Dakota did the Mentos and Diet Coke experiment, which makes a reliable explosion. The Diet Coke made a huge mess. It got all over Torpse's windows. When Torpse saw it, I wished as hard as I could for the invisibility superpower.

We tried to clean the windows, but we couldn't reach them. Mom had to buy a ladder. She docked Dakota's allowance to cover the cost. I don't have any allowance coming either, because I took an advance to buy new tennis balls, which are already used up. So no new tennis balls and no allowance for the rest of the year.

"Children! Children!" Mr. Torpse is standing on his tiny porch. He's aiming his cane at us and squinting behind his glasses.

"Mr. Torpse, Mr. Torpse!" Izzy hops up and down. "Hi, Mr. Torpse!"

Mr. Torpse frowns at her. "Hello."

"He said hi. I go hug him?" But before we have time to answer, Izzy runs up to Mr. Torpse's porch and gives him a big hug.

"Oh, for goodness' sake." Mr. Torpse tries to right his glasses.

"Thank you, Mr. Torpse! Thank you! Thank you!" Izzy waves as she runs back to us.

"For what?" he calls.

"Hugs!" Izzy says.

"But the police!" He thumps his cane on the rolled-up yoga mat leaning against the railing. "What did they say?"

"The police good, Mr. Torpse!" Izzy shouts.

"But, but . . . ," he sputters.

"The firemen are good too. Do you like the firemen, Mr. Torpse?" Izzy asks.

"There was a fire?" Mr. Torpse cries.

"No. No. She just said she likes firemen," I tell him.

Mr. Torpse scowls at me.

"How did he know about the police?" I whisper to Dakota.

"Somebody must have told him," Dakota hisses.

Mr. Torpse takes off his slipper. I think he's going to slap it against the porch rail like he does when he gets mad. But he just stands there. "You children!" he shouts.

"Yes, sir," I say.

"Tell your mother I want to speak with her. Tell her to find her lease. I'll be down tomorrow morning at eight."

Does he have to shout so loud all the neighbors hear? It's scary when your landlord gets mad at you. Landlord trouble is worse than flunking a test, because landlords don't give retakes.

"I'll tell her," I say.

Dakota skips up next to me. "What's a lease?"

"It's a paper you sign when you rent an apartment."

"I don't get it," Dakota says. "Why would you sign a paper to live in your home?"

"Because we don't own it. Torpse does."

"Yeah, but it's our home, not his." Dakota says.

"Actually, it's not," I say.

"Torpse has his home and we have ours."

"Nope. He owns both of them."

"That's not fair," Dakota says.

I shrug.

"Our home." Izzy waits by the door, smiling at us. "Mommy said."

5

DESPERATELY SEEKING GEEKS

The next morning, when we open the door, a bag of kitty litter is sitting outside in a plastic box with a note attached.

Dakota grins.

We get the kitty-litter box set up and put it on the patio with Cupcake. We need to teach her to use it, but there's no time right now.

I pull on my hoodie and grab Izzy's hand, and the three of us take off. The weather is starting to turn. A light mist is falling. It sits like a roof on my hair.

We pass Mr. Torpse in weird black stretchy pants heading down our stairs to talk to Mom. "Uh-oh," Dakota says as she hops on the landing with her polka-dot backpack.

"Hi, Mr. Torpse." Izzy waves. Then she runs up to him and hands him something. When she gets back, I ask her: "What did you give him?"

"Money," Izzy says.

"Monopoly money?"

She nods.

"What do you think Torpse will say?" Dakota asks me.

"He'll probably tell Mom not to let you blow things up."

Dakota groans. "How am I supposed to cure cancer if I can't practice?"

"Cure cancer? By exploding watermelons?"

"It's a start, Liam. Think about it. If I cure cancer, we'll never have to worry about money again. But I'll need help."

"Really? I can't imagine why," I say sarcastically.

"We *have* money," Izzy says.

The bus stop is at the top of the hill. There are three girls up there already. When Izzy sees them, she pulls free and runs the rest of the way up. The three girls all hug her. They're younger than she is, but she doesn't care. For Izzy, friendship is contagious.

Dakota rattles on. I tune back in.

"My club is going to help me."

"Your what?"

"Remember? Mom told me to start a club."

Dakota doesn't have "mates," as my mom calls them. The only time Dakota ever has kids over that aren't my friends or Izzy's friends, Mom has invited them. Friends your mom makes for you are not the same as real friends.

I look around, hoping to see Dodge, but I don't expect to. Most of the time Crash drives him.

Dakota has a dreamy look. "Everybody is going to want to join. Who doesn't want to be a rich nerd with a finish-up?"

"A finish-up? What's that?"

Dakota juts her chin out. "A finish-up, Liam. You know . . . a company that makes a lot of money."

"Oh, you mean a start-up?"

"Oh. Yeah." Dakota nods, unzipping her backpack and pulling out seven pink wristbands made from torn-up pink tutus. "Every kid who gets ninety-seven point five or better on our science test will receive one of these."

"Ninety-seven point five?"

"They can miss one," she explains.

"Generous of you."

"Mrs. Johnson makes mistakes."

"Oh, so they're allowed to miss one *if it's your teacher's fault*?" I ask as the bus rumbles around the corner. "When are you planning on giving those out?"

She picks her backpack up. "At recess. That's when the Glitter Nerds meet."

"Glitter Nerds . . . Is that what you're going to call them? You're not inviting any boys, are you? Because boys don't like glitter."

"Mom said boys can wear glitter if they want to."

"Mom is an expert on this?"

Dakota nods. "We're going to meet at the big library table."

"Nobody goes to the library at recess."

"Nerds do." Dakota gets in line in front of me.

The bus stops with a hissing *phooof* and the door flaps open. I keep an eye on Izzy, who is holding hands with the little girls. They get on first.

"Those are one hundred percent nerds. What you need are partial nerds."

Dakota frowns at me. "I'm not a partial."

"Tell me about it."

"Well, it's better if nobody but us goes to the library." She bangs her backpack—*bump, bump, bump*—onto the bus. "Then it won't be hard to get a table."

✳

Once we get to school, Dakota and I walk Izzy to her class. At home, Izzy's size doesn't seem unusual. She's only seven. But when she's with the other second graders, I see how small she is.

As soon as we drop Izzy off, I start ignoring Dakota. Nobody in fifth grade talks to anyone in third grade, for obvious reasons. But there are a couple of guys on my tennis team who, through no fault of their own, are in Dakota's class. I can't believe there are third graders good enough for our team, but there are. I'd rather my sister didn't ask them to wear a pink-tutu wristband, because guys on your team are important. Being on a team isn't a super-power, but it's close.

Later, at recess, I can't keep myself from swinging past the library on my way to the Ga-ga pit. Ga-ga is like dodgeball, only better. Everybody plays it around here.

Through the window, I spot Dakota at a table with her pile of pink wristbands.

A couple of fifth-grade girls walk by wearing wolf ears. They don't go in.

A girl is in the back of the library, reading. She doesn't look up. And then another girl walks by, the little sister of a guy I know.

Great. She'll probably tell her brother she saw me standing by myself outside the library.

Two guys walk in. Dakota waves at them. They run in the other direction. Dakota slinks down in her chair.

I can't watch. If I'm standing here, people will remember this is my sister. I head for the Ga-ga pit, where I get nailed. Immediately. Dakota's messing with my mojo.

I wait for my turn to get back in. I'm almost up when it occurs to me that it might be better to exercise damage control. I head back to the library and peek in the window. Dakota's still there, only now there's a pink wristband in front of each empty chair and she is under the table.

"Liam?" Dodge calls from the fifth-grade garden. I motion for him to come over. He looks in the library window and then shakes his head. "We can't let that go on," he mumbles. We push through the library door.

"Dakota, what are you doing down there?" I ask.

"No one came," Dakota says in a squashed-down voice.

"Did you show the video before class?" I ask.

She nods.

"That's strange," Dodge says. "I told some kids about the exploding watermelon. Everyone liked it."

Dakota's eyes glow. "You told *fifth graders*?"

Dodge nods. "I bet the third graders didn't really understand. It's more of a fifth-grade thing."

Dakota's face lights up like a phosphorescent fish.

"Me and Liam want to join," Dodge says.

Dakota frowns. "Liam doesn't want to."

Dodge kneels down. "He told me he did, but he was afraid to tell you. Right, Liam?"

I chomp the inside of my cheek but I nod yes.

Dakota's blue eyes shine. She gets out from under the table and ties a pink band around Dodge's wrist and one around mine.

"Let's go play Ga-ga," Dodge says.

I look at Dakota. I can't exactly let her stand here looking pathetic for the rest of recess. "You too," I mumble.

"They don't let third graders in the Ga-ga pit," Dakota says.

"They will if you're with us," I say.

A little gasp comes out of Dakota. She scoops up the wristbands and trots after us.

6

A PINK BRACELET . . . DUDE?

In science, I'm quietly doing my worksheet when Mr. Gupta calls my name. Mr. Gupta teaches science to fourth and fifth grade. He also teaches PE, and he's my tennis coach.

Why's he calling me? We don't usually talk about tennis in class. Maybe my project. I'm putting together a genealogy chart with the heights of all my family members.

Now I have to walk by everyone to where Mr. Gupta is perched on top of the squeaky Styrofoam Earth. Mr. Gupta always has a display in the front of the classroom. Last month it was a tornado with tiny plastic houses and cows and cars stuck to it. Now it's models of the planets.

Mr. Gupta is never embarrassed by stuff like this. I don't know why. Still, he's my favorite teacher.

Everybody watches me go to the front of the class. Are they jealous I get one-on-one Gupta time?

"Have a seat, Liam." He points to Saturn but I don't want to sit on a planet that has rings like it's wearing a skirt. I choose Jupiter. Nobody makes fun of a guy who sits on Jupiter.

"Liam, could you explain to me please about your sister?" Mr. Gupta asks.

Uh-oh. "My sister, sir?" I mumble.

"Yes, your sister Dakota Rose. Yesterday we were playing junior basketball, a good game with the half-size hoops. Your sister was under the bleachers. She would not come out. She said before she can play, she must know why the rubber in the basketball is not on the Periodic Table of the Elements."

My cheeks get hot. I look around to see if anyone heard. Moses is searching in his desk for something. Dodge is chewing on his pencil. Everyone else is working.

Mr. Gupta leans over, his turban tipping forward. "Is she messing with me?"

"No, sir." I shake my head.

"She really wants to know?"

I nod.

"All right, then. I will explain to her. And, Liam, what does she do to make the other children run away?"

My voice drops below a whisper. "I don't even know where to begin."

"I see." He lifts his glasses onto his forehead and rubs his eyes. "And you, Liam, how are you doing on your family chart?"

"Oh—on my mom's side . . . I don't know much about the Aussies," I say.

He nods. "It is just an indication, Liam. We do not know for sure. And remember there are tennis players who are not tall. Bobby Riggs was five feet seven."

"Who is he?"

"Before your time. Will you be at practice?"

"Yes, sir."

When I'm back in my seat, Dodge leans over. "What did Gupta want?"

I wouldn't mind telling him, but not with everyone listening. I shrug. Dodge nods.

A kid with two-tone hair leans across the aisle and grabs my wristband. "What's this?"

I beckon with my finger. "Dodge and I were jumped," I whisper in his ear.

The kid looks over at Dodge. Dodge nods.

"By who?"

"Strange girls."

"Really?" Two-tone hair squints. He leans over to tell Moses.

Like I was saying, Moses is cool. The way he walks. The way he talks. The apps he has. The music. The videos he's seen before everyone else.

Moses cocks his head at me. "Can't you take it off now?"

"You got to keep it on or they'll do it again," I explain.

"Dude? A pink bracelet?" Moses asks.

"You got a sister, man?" I ask.

Moses sticks three fingers in the air. "I got three."

"They ever bug you?"

"Does a dog take a whiz on three legs?" Moses asks.

I turn red. Does he know about Cupcake? He can't, can he? I shake my wristband in his face. "Keeps them from bugging me."

Moses smiles. "I'll wear pink bracelets, pink tights, and a tiara if it'll keep my sisters away."

I laugh. He laughs. We rap knuckles, Moses and I.

I thought guys didn't do that anymore. But if Moses does it, it's done.

✳

I don't see Moses again until after-school tennis-team practice.

This is our first practice this year, but already I can tell how different it will be from last year.

There are a lot more guys and one more girl, for one thing. There are two third graders on the team, and four fifth graders; everyone else is in middle school. Middle school!

Mr. Gupta starts off with the geometry of tennis: how to work the angles when you play. Then he tells us how important it is not to miss any practices, and he gets a big basket of balls and begins drilling us.

We take turns hitting approach shots, volleys, and smash overheads. Dodge and I have had practice with these shots because Crash is a good teacher.

I watch everyone hit to figure out who the best player is. It's clearly Moses. He's even better than the middle school kids!

I wish we could keep on doing drills forever, that's how fun it is. I will never in a million years miss a practice, and I can't imagine why anyone else would either.

Dodge and I hit together, which we are used to doing. Out of the corner of my eye, I see Moses hitting with a guy named Will. I want to stand and watch. That's how good Moses is. Boy, will it be fun to play against him.

Practice is over way too soon. "Nice job today, Liam," Mr. Gupta says when I'm picking up balls.

He probably said "nice job" to lots of people. Moses probably got a "great job."

I'm just walking out when Moses catches up with me.

"Hey, Liam, can I get your cell number?"

"Sure." I rattle it off to him, like it's no big thing.

He enters my number into his phone. Then he gives me his number, but Dakota's got the cell, so I just remember it.

I say it in my head over and over again the whole way home.

7

PHONE-SWEAR

On Wednesday when we get home, the carpet-cleaning machine is parked by the door. Mom is cleaning up after Cupcake again. Cupcake winds around our legs. She sticks her nose in my face and slops her licks everywhere.

I swear she loves me best, but Dakota thinks it's her.

We take Cupcake onto the patio and try to show her how to use the kitty-litter box. Dakota squats down in the box like she's a dog peeing, but Cupcake shows no interest. We try to get Cupcake to squat. But her legs won't bend.

Then I get treats and bury them in the kitty litter.

This gets her attention, and she jumps into the

box and begins pawing for the treats, which tips the tray over, dumping the kitty litter out.

I get the broom from my mom, who is trying hard not to laugh.

Once we get the kitty litter back in the box, we pick the box up and take Cupcake for a walk. We know where she likes to do her business, so we'll put the box there just before.

But the box is heavy to lug. And Cupcake pees before I can get it under her.

When we get back home, we leave the kitty-litter

box outside and I ask Mom: "How did it go with Mr. Torpse?"

Mom sighs. "He isn't one to cut us slack, I'll tell you that. Stay off the carpet. It's still a little wet."

"What did he say?"

"He came in mad about the explosion and left mad about Cupcake."

Cupcake's head is heavy in my hand as I scratch under her chin. Her eyes are half closed.

Mom leans down and wipes the dog hair off her pants. "I had her on the patio, but then she started barking. You know how Mr. Torpse hates that. So I brought her in and she peed right at his feet. Any closer and his slippers would have been soaked."

"She doesn't like him. That's for sure. What did he say?"

"He said get rid of her."

"No!" I say. "Did you explain she's got, you know, a medical condition?"

"Mr. Torpse is not interested in our dog's medical condition."

"But there's no way we're getting rid of Cupcake."

My mom climbs up on the step stool to reach the serving trays. She seesaws her head. "We'll find her a good home. A place where she'll have her own yard. She'll be an outside dog." She swallows hard.

"At least let us try the kitty litter."

"You've been trying the kitty litter," Mom says as Cupcake turns round and round, then plops on the floor by Mom's feet.

Dakota is back inside now.

Mom sets the trays down. "We have to do what's right for Cupcake."

"What's right for Cupcake is staying with us," Dakota declares.

I remember how happy Cupcake was playing in our old yard. Then I think about how, the second I'm upset, she comes running. She can tell how I'm feeling before anyone else.

"You'll give us a chance, right?" I whisper, when Dakota goes into the bathroom.

"Yes," Mom says.

"Can't we take her back to the vet?"

"I've called the vet several times. She says there's nothing more they can do for her unless we take her to UC Davis for special tests."

I kneel down by Cupcake, rubbing her belly. Her paws are flapping in the air and her tongue is lolling out to one side.

"Look," Mom whispers, "don't get Dakota wound up about this. I don't have time to deal with her right now. This is between us, right?"

"Right," I say.

That's the trouble with being the oldest. I know things my sisters don't. It's a lot of responsibility. I get Cupcake's leash and pick up the litter box, but she goes on a sit-down strike. She is not about to pee in that thing.

I try to think logically. What can we do about Cupcake's problem?

Maybe she's forgotten her house training. Maybe it's as simple as reminding her again.

I find her treats and cut them into tiny pieces. Then I take her on a walk, and when she pees, I give her a treat. "Good dog," I say. Cupcake wags her tail.

Back at home, Mom is getting ready for the Forty-Sevens' party tonight. The Forty-Sevens all have Down syndrome, like Izzy, which means they have an extra chromosome. Forty-seven chromosomes, in total. Most everyone else has forty-six.

Our apartment isn't big enough for all the Forty-Sevens. Plus, it's hard to find parking on our street. But the Forty-Sevens and their parents don't mind. All the Forty-Sevens' parents are big huggers. Some of the kids are huggers like Izzy, but most of them just say hello.

I've finished hosing down the patio when I hear my old phone buzzing in Dakota and Izzy's room.

The text is from Dodge. He wants to come over; otherwise he has to go with Crash to the Sisters in Crime mystery writers' meeting. He's told me about those meetings before. He says the other members are sweet old ladies who argue about who has a better way to murder people. Crash is their resident expert.

Sometimes they meet at Fiorelli's. That's how Mom met Crash and I met Dodge.

I text him a thumbs-up and return the phone to Dakota's bed.

Then I get back to thinking up ways to make money. A bake sale? But how are we going to get the money for the ingredients? We could offer to do chores for the neighbors. Or call Dad and beg for our birthday money early. Maybe we could make a hundred dollars that way, but three thousand? Never.

Dakota and I are filling the drinks barrel with ice when Izzy points to our pink wristbands. "May I have?"

Dakota runs the ice-cube tray under hot water to get the last pieces out. "I'm going to make a blue one for you. Blue is special."

Izzy shakes her head. "Pink."

"No," Dakota says.

"Why?" Izzy asks.

"Because it's not the right color for you."

"Why?"

Dakota gets another tray out of the freezer. "Because it isn't, that's all."

Izzy frowns at her. "Am smart," she says.

"It's *my* club! I get to make the rules." Dakota taps her chest.

"Shut up, Dakota." I take off my band and fasten it around Izzy's wrist.

Izzy runs to the mirror to admire herself with the pink wristband. Her smile could melt Antarctica.

I glare at Dakota. "Don't be mean to Izzy."

"I wasn't."

"Not letting her be a member, what do you think that is?"

Dakota's face puckers up like she ate a lemon rind.

"Anyway," I say, "we've got bigger problems."

"Like what?" Dakota asks.

"I'm not supposed to tell you until after. Mom doesn't want you to get all wound up."

"I won't get all wound up."

"Phone swear?"

Dakota nods.

"Text it," I tell her.

Dakota takes out the phone and texts her promise to Dodge.

If I get wound up, Liam gets the phone.

Dodge is used to this. We always text him our phone swears.

"If we don't figure out how to get Cupcake to stop peeing everywhere," I say, "then Mom's going to get rid of her."

"She won't. She loves Cupcake."

"Torpse said she had to."

Dakota leans back on the couch, twirling her glitter nerds wristband, thinking so hard I can see the processing icon spinning around on her face.

"We'll get my nerd herd to help." She smiles.

"You changed your club name?"

"On account of you and Dodge," she admits.

"Really?" Dakota never changes anything. Once she decides something, it's set, like your birthday.

"Dodge is coming over, right?" Dakota asks.

"Right," I say.

Then Izzy and I go outside to wait for the Forty-Sevens. It's early, but she gets excited when her friends come over.

Maybe this is weird, but I like it when they visit too. I have fun around them, like I did back in second grade, when no one noticed what you did.

We watch as a sleek gray car pulls up in the driveway. A lady in a red flowered dress gets out and knocks on Torpse's door.

Mr. Torpse comes out dressed in regular clothes, with wet comb marks in his hair.

When they get in the lady's car, Izzy starts running toward them.

"Izzy, wait!" I shout as she dives for something on the pavement.

"Mr. Torpse! Mr. Torpse!" she cries, waving a red scarf at the car window.

Mr. Torpse presses down the window. "What?" he growls.

"Why, aren't you a dear." The lady leans over Mr. Torpse and takes the scarf. "Thank you, honey."

Izzy is smiling when she comes back to me. She doesn't talk clearly, and people sometimes say peculiar things to Mom, like *You've been chosen for this special blessing.*

Izzy has to try ten times harder than we do at school. Even simple things like opening the door with a key can be challenging. But honestly, I think the extra chromosome makes her nicer.

I once overheard Mom say she thinks Dakota's endless crazy ideas have something to do with Izzy. Dakota sees how hard Izzy tries and doesn't want to be outdone.

"I'm glad Torpse went out," I tell Izzy. We don't need him coming down to complain we're making too much noise when the Forty-Sevens are here."

Izzy smiles. "Torpse the Corpse."

The first of the Forty-Sevens, Beatrice and her mom, arrive and we take them inside. Then Dodge and more Forty-Sevens come in.

Now everyone is saying hello and pouring apple cider and taking the tinfoil off the potluck plates. I head for Dakota and Izzy's room to find the ukulele.

Catalina, who has pierced ears and a dozen braids, sees Izzy's wristband. She runs her fingers over it. "Pretty."

"You want one?" Izzy asks, looking over at Dakota. Dakota shakes her head a hair-whipping no.

Izzy unzips Dakota's backpack and pulls out the pink wristbands.

Dakota's eyes get big. She is about to yell at Izzy, but I shake my head no. Then I point to a pink chair. She makes a face, but she sits down to give herself

a time-out. Even she knows not to make a scene at the Forty-Sevens' party.

Now everybody has a pink tutu wristband. The bands are a hit.

We even come up with a pink-armband salute. We all crouch in a huddle; then we jump up and shoot our band hands in the air. It's pretty fun.

8

NERD POWER

When they call "Dinnertime," Dakota doesn't move from the pink chair. She's still mad.

After we've cleaned our plates, we go outside on the driveway and Izzy and DeShawn water Izzy's plants. Izzy, Dakota, and Mom planted flowers in mason jars, but Dakota's are dead. She said she already understands photosynthesis, thank you very much.

Izzy and I play with the big ball and the giant Frisbee. Izzy throws and catches okay because she practices a lot. But some of the Forty-Sevens have more trouble, so we play with extra-large stuff.

Then we go back inside and I pick up the ukulele. I only know a few chords, so mostly I strum and Dodge sings. He sings better than I do. The Forty-Sevens sing along and Emilio dances. I try to mimic his steps and everybody laughs. It's a relief to be around the Forty-Sevens. They don't judge.

Dodge and I make up a song. It takes us a while but we finally come up with something we like. We sing the first line, and everyone else sings it after us.

"Raise your hand
(Raise your hand)
Shake the band
(Shake the band.)
Make a tower
(Make a tower)
Of nerdy power
(Of nerdy power.)
We're the herd
(We're the herd)
Of the nerd
(Of the nerd.)

We have your back
(We have your back)
And that's a fact, Jack.
(And that's a fact, Jack.)"

While we sing, we stand in a circle and raise our wristband arms. Then we make a tower of fists, and when the song is over, everybody fist-bumps.

The Forty-Sevens go wild. They love this.

The next time we sing the song, Dakota has turned the chair around so she can see. By the fourth time, she's joined the circle and is singing with us.

"Who is Jack?" Izzy asks.

"'Jack' is just made up because it rhymes."

Beatrice's mom sticks her head in the door. "Time to go."

"Mommy, look." Beatrice shows her mom the pink wristband. "I'm in the Nerd Herd."

"The what?"

"It's a club for nerds."

Beatrice's mom stares at Dakota, Dodge, and me.

"Just a minute," she tells Beatrice.

"Yay! I-can-stay! Yay! Yay! Yay!" Beatrice shouts.

Now we go back to singing our usual songs about octopus gardens and rooms without a roof, until Mom comes back.

"Liam," she whispers, beckoning with her finger. "A nerd club? *Really?* You're not making fun of them, are you?"

"No! It's just that Dakota tried to start a nerd club at school, only nobody came. So me and Dodge became members." I show her the pink wristbands. "And Izzy wanted a wristband and then everybody else did too."

"Oh." Mom nods, chewing her lip. "Why'd she start the club in the first place?"

"*I* started it. *Me. Not Liam!*" Dakota interrupts.

"That's what I said, Dakota. Jeez," I tell her.

"You told me to start a recess club to meet kids like me even if there aren't any. I'm not a partial nerd. I'm one hundred percent," Dakota says to Mom.

Mom nods.

"We need money for the vet. I thought the kids at school could help me think of a way to get it," Dakota explains.

"For the vet." Mom glares at me.

"This was before he told me," Dakota says.

"Before he told you what?" Mom asks.

I roll my eyes. Then I put out my hand for the phone.

"Wait, wait, I didn't get wound up," Dakota says.

"Yeah, but you told."

Dakota sighs. She digs the phone out of her pocket and hands it to me.

Mom shakes her head.

"You can't give Cupcake away, Mom," Dakota says. "We all love her and so do you."

"I know that, honey." Mom runs her hands tenderly over Dakota's hair. "We'll get through this. All of us together."

"Together means Cupcake too," Dakota insists.

My mom sighs. "I hope so. I really do."

I hand Dodge the ukulele, then get a few more treats and take Cupcake out again.

When I get back, Mom is cleaning up a yellow puddle by the patio door.

I get down to Cupcake's level and look her in the eye. "When'd you do that?"

She gives me a small apologetic lick.

"Seriously . . . you can't do that anymore, all right?"

Her deep brown eyes stare back at me. She does understand, doesn't she?

9

WHAT I DO FOR FRIED RICE

"**M**om," I say on Friday morning when she's scooping homemade applesauce into bowls. "You're not going to give Cupcake away without telling us, are you?"

"Of course not." She sets the bowls in front of us.

"How much time do we have?"

"Mr. Torpse gave us three weeks, but that was two days ago."

"Three weeks!" Dakota yells.

"I don't like it any better than you do," she says, and then turns to Izzy. "Use your spoon, please." Izzy likes to start every meal with a taste on her finger.

Mom kneels down, runs her hand over Cupcake's head, and scratches under her chin. Cupcake puts her paw over Mom's hand so it won't ever move again.

"I'll take her out every five minutes," I say.

"Every minute! Every second!" Dakota yells.

"I know!" Izzy waves her spoon in the air. "We make a toilet-shaped rug."

"Gross, Izzy," Dakota says.

"You're gross," Izzy says. "You keep my pee in the peanut butter jar."

I laugh. "Good one, Izzy," I say.

"Wait, wait, wait. I have an idea, but it's a secret." Dakota is wearing a sparkly pink striped shirt and boots that look like slippers. She's so excited she jumps out of her seat.

Mom and I exchange a look. The last time Dakota had a secret idea, she shaved off her eyebrows to see if they served a purpose on her face. And then the school nurse called my mother. And since there is only one school nurse for the whole county, that was a big deal.

Mom sighs. "Do you want to tell us a little about your idea?"

Dakota gives a wild shake of her bed-hair head. "Nope."

✳

After breakfast, Dakota, Izzy, and I head for the bus stop.

I'm hoping Dakota will forget about her nerd club now and go back to doing whatever she did before at recess. Something no one will notice. Aren't nerds supposed to be quiet?

On the bus, I notice Dakota's mouth is moving. Oh, great. Now she's talking to herself.

At school Dodge and I discuss my Bigfoot collection. I have the best one of anyone I know. Okay, maybe it's the only collection of anyone I know, but still. Bigfoot is a giant hairy guy who hides in the forest.

Dakota is always telling me there's no proof that Bigfoot exists. Izzy believes, though. She gets as excited as I do if anyone finds a new footprint.

Dodge and I are discussing this when Moses walks by.

"Bigfoot?" Moses asks.

"Yeah."

"You ever see him?"

I shake my head. Everybody always asks this. I

mean, I've never seen a dinosaur either, but I know they existed because there are bones. We don't exactly have bones of Bigfoot, but still.

"Do you think he's related to the two-legged bear?" Moses asks.

"What two-legged bear?"

"You haven't seen the two-legged bear?" Moses whips out his phone. He has a brand-new smartphone. I have the only stupid phone left in the universe. "You have to see this." He types in something, and then hands the phone to me. Dodge, Moses, and a few other kids crowd around.

There he is . . . a real, live, normal bear—not a man in a bear suit—walking on two legs like a man. Even his posture looks like a man's. But he's a bear.

The more times we watch, the more sure we become that this bear is for real.

"Can I see your Bigfoot things?" Moses asks.

"Sure."

"I've seen you out walking," Moses says. "You live near my aunt."

"Oh. Yeah." I try to smile but my lips bend the wrong way.

"Can I come over sometime?" Moses asks.

"Uhhh, well, I'll bring it all to school." The last thing I want is for Moses to come to my basement apartment with the rickety stairs and the broken screens and the rusted-out washing machine. Who has a washing machine in their yard?

I'm betting Moses has one mom and one dad who both live together in one house with a garage and a garage door and a yard with trees and leaves. They probably have a leaf blower and a garage-door opener and maybe even a tennis court.

I think back to when we had a house. I wonder who lives in our house now? Whoever he is . . . I hate him.

✳

Dodge and I are just finishing lunch when Mom texts me.

Tell Dakota to stay after school for the maker fair meeting and please go with her. Pick you up at 4. I owe you . . . fried rice?

I have to go with her to a meeting for third graders? I can hardly wait.

When Dodge and I find Dakota and I tell her what Mom texted, she nods. "Mom wants me to find other kids like me."

"There are no kids *like you.*"

"Yeah, I know." She grins.

"Maybe if you could be a little less nerdy."

"I like my whole nerdiness." She hugs herself. "You're only one-third nerd." She shakes her head. "It's not enough."

I roll my eyes. Then I look hopefully at Dodge. "You want to come?"

Dodge smiles like I offered him chocolate cake. The good kind. No beets.

I swear I could invite Dodge over for one of Dad's insurance talks and he'd be happy about it. He is a great friend.

We are headed for Dakota's third-grade classroom when Moses calls to us.

"Hey, where you guys going?"

"Nowhere, um, important," I say.

"To my classroom. Want to come?" Dakota asks.

"Sure," he says.

"You're Moses, right?" she says. "My brother is always talking about you."

My cheeks get hot. Why does she do this to me?

We slip in the door of room 23. Dakota already has her hand raised and she's whipping it all around. Mrs. Johnson is rattling off the rules. Mr. Gupta is sitting quietly, the tips of his fingers together.

He's here too? He doesn't teach third graders.

Dodge swoops by the cookie table, and then he joins Moses, me, and Dakota in the back row with six molasses cookies with frosting hard as asphalt and homemade M&M's-covered brownies. We are busy stuffing our faces when Mrs. Johnson tells Dakota, "We'll take questions later."

Dakota's arm drops like a boulder.

A second later it shoots up again.

"Dakota," Mrs. Johnson sighs.

"You didn't say how much later."

The only other people raising hands are parents. A dad in a business suit with a clump of hair growing from his chin and two pierced ears has a question about who the judges will be. Mrs. Johnson is careful to avoid eye contact with Dakota and her windmill arm, which isn't easy.

A mom with dreadlocks and big red glasses says, "I think there's a child with a question." She points to Dakota, who pops out of her seat.

"Are we eligible for other prizes besides the maker fair prizes?"

"Other prizes?" Mrs. Johnson asks.

"Scholarships or things with money," Dakota answers. "My dad says I need money to go to college. And we need money for our dog."

I slink down in my chair. Now Mr. Gupta—not to mention Moses—is going to know we have money problems.

"No scholarships." Mrs. Johnson's smile looks stiff. She points to another parent with his hand raised.

Dakota's arm pops up again. "What about prize money?"

"The winner of our maker fair award will represent Red Horse Elementary in a county-wide competition. Whoever wins that will receive five hundred dollars."

Dakota grins.

"Dakota, do you have a parent with you today?" Mrs. Johnson looks out hopefully at the grown-ups.

"Just my brother, Liam—" Dakota points at me.

My hand is low, barely off my lap. I wave, lamely wishing for spray-on invisibility. Apply once and Dakota disappears for the entire school day. Why isn't Mom or Dad here?

I glance sideways at Moses.

"And my friend Dodge. And that's Moses." Dakota points to Dodge, who has a brownie in his mouth, then to Moses.

"Ahh . . . well, perhaps your brother will see me once we're done with the questions here."

There is not enough fried rice in the world for this.

"How about five *thousand* dollars," Dakota says.

"Excuse me?" Mrs. Johnson asks.

"Forgive me, Mrs. Johnson," Mr. Gupta says, "but I may be able to help Dakota. She is always thinking. This is a good quality in a third grader."

Mrs. Johnson smiles at Mr. Gupta like he has just offered her a trip to Hawaii.

"Dakota Rose. Perhaps you will want to work with another student on your maker fair entry," Mr. Gupta says.

"No thank you," Dakota says. "I don't want to share the prize money."

What is the matter with her? Why can't she just say yes? I steal a look at Moses.

"Ahh," Mr. Gupta says. "I had thought you were interested in being a scientist."

"I am a scientist."

"Scientists work in teams. Do you know why you have two eyes, Dakota?"

"The other is a spare like my mom has an extra tire in the trunk."

All the parents laugh. I slink down lower in my seat.

"Yes, though there is another reason." His pointer

finger sticks up in the air. "You cannot perceive depth, Dakota Rose, with just one eye. Two is not just double one; it enables you to see in an entirely new way."

Dakota's never been on a team. She doesn't know a team is way stronger than a bunch of people together.

"Just consider it." Mr. Gupta points to his temple. "And bring me your ideas tomorrow in PE class and we will plan."

Bring *him* her ideas? Why doesn't he say bring Mrs. Johnson her ideas? Dakota better not take over Mr. Gupta too.

But after the meeting, Mr. Gupta doesn't talk to Dakota; he talks to Moses, Dodge, and me. "Have you been practicing your sprints and your serve toss?"

We nod.

"Keep your elbow straight. The ball must go to that one spot. You must picture in your mind the spot."

"Yes, sir," we say. But now I see Mrs. Johnson watching me.

"Hello, Dakota's brother," she says. "Liam, right?"

I nod, my face getting hot.

She smiles warmly at me. "Must be challenging."

"Yes, ma'am."

"Your parents are coming to Back-to-School Night?"

"Yes."

"Tell them to come talk to me."

"Yes, ma'am."

"Nice to meet you, Liam. I appreciate your coming along with your sister today. Mr. Gupta speaks highly of you."

Mr. Gupta talks about me in the teachers' lounge?

"Please tell your mother we all really like Dakota. We're just hoping she can learn to take it down a notch."

I nod. "Dakota wears you out."

Mrs. Johnson laughs. "Yes, she does."

But all I can think about is: *Mr. Gupta speaks highly of me!*

*✳ **10** ✳*

BIGFOOT AND THE TWO-LEGGED BEAR

Today Mom takes Izzy to speech therapy and Dad takes her to the eye doctor, so Crash is at our house when we get there. Crash has a slow walk and a calm way about him. The only thing that isn't calm is the crazy hair growing out of his ears, as if whatever he's hearing has gotten his hair all upset.

"Everything okay with Izzy?" Crash asks.

"They're picking up her new glasses," I say.

"I thought your mom wasn't sure she needed them."

"She got a second opinion."

"Hope Izzy keeps track of them better than I do. I'm thinking of getting one of those pearly chains like the ladies wear. Be the talk of the station." He grins.

"Hey, Crash," I say. "How much does it cost to buy a house?"

He squints at me. "You in the market?"

"Not exactly."

Crash nods. I can tell he knows what I'm thinking. I still kind of hope my parents will get back together again. Dad doesn't have a girlfriend anymore and Mom doesn't have a boyfriend, so now is the time.

"Only couple I know got remarried . . . it didn't turn out well," Crash says.

"Was it a homicide?" I ask.

He laughs. "No, nothing like that."

"My parents love each other," I announce.

"Doesn't mean they can live together."

"Why not?"

Crash shrugs. "People got to work things out their own way. Our job is to let them."

"Maybe they just haven't thought of it."

Crash picks up a plate of cookies and offers me one. "Somehow, Liam, I don't think that's it."

I look at the cookies. "What kind?"

"Chocolate and chili powder."

"Crash . . . ," Dodge groans, shaking his head as we go to my room.

"Trying something new. Don't want to get set in my ways," he calls after us.

Once my door is closed, Dakota and I hand our cookies to Dodge. Then Dodge plops down in the chair in front of the Xbox.

"Hey, Dodge, how come you live with your grandpa anyway? Where's your mom?" Dakota asks.

"SHUT UP, Dakota!" I say.

Dodge shoves two cookies in his mouth. "She's fishing."

Dakota cocks her head. "What about at night? She couldn't be fishing at night!"

Dodge wipes the crumbs off his mouth. "I don't know."

"How could you *not know*?" Dakota asks.

I step on Dakota's toe and give it a good grind. She clamps her mouth shut.

If Roger Federer had Dakota as a sister, he'd never win another match.

Dakota marches out to Crash.

"Where is Dodge's mom?"

"Oh no!" I plunk down on the bed.

"That is not your business, Dakota," Crash says.

"It is so. Dodge is my friend."

"Some things you have to let people tell you in their own time. Friendship is a gentle thing. More like catching a bird then forcing a stuck drawer closed."

Dakota's lower lip puckers out.

"Oh, Dakota." He folds her into a big hug.

Now she's back in my room. She smiles at Dodge and that's the end of it.

I open the closet door and feel around the top shelf, which is where I keep my Bigfoot stuff. I want to put it in my backpack so I don't forget to take it to school to show Moses tomorrow. But I can't reach any of it, so I roll my desk chair over to the closet and climb on. I can't wait until I'm tall enough to reach without the chair.

Cans of old tennis balls, wadded-up gym shorts, a flat basketball, an old jar with my baby teeth and website passwords are up there, but no Bigfoot stuff.

"Dakota, have you seen my Bigfoot things—my mug and photo and pencil?"

Dakota and Dodge are both focused on the Xbox now. Dakota nods.

"Where are they?"

"Gone," she mumbles.

"Gone? Gone where?"

"Alabama."

"What?"

Dakota scratches her head. "We all had to make a contribution. You know, for Cupcake."

"What's that have to do with Bigfoot?"

"I sold everything on eBay. We made thirty dollars on it. I never thought we'd get that much for your stupid old Bigfoot stuff." She beams.

"You didn't ask me! You can't sell my things."

"But you love Cupcake. And anyway, scientists don't believe in Bigfoot. How come there aren't two footprints, or four, or ten? They always find one. Nobody walks around with just one foot. Have you tried it?" She hops around my room. "It doesn't work."

I cross my arms and stare at her. "Izzy and I like Bigfoot. We don't care what you think."

"I thought you'd be happy. Don't you care about Cupcake?" She sighs. Then she hops over to cardboard Roger Federer and taps his chest. "I was going to sell Roger but I didn't think he'd fold down small enough to get in the box."

"Don't touch Roger!" I shout, and Cupcake comes running to see what the excitement is all about.

Dodge can't concentrate on the Xbox anymore. He looks down at his shoes. Cupcake stands between us, shaking.

"Why didn't you sell your own stuff?" I ask.

"I did. I sold my purple sequin slippers and Izzy's horse collection."

"No!" I gasp. "You didn't sell Izzy's horses!"

"It's not for me. It's for Cupcake." Dakota runs her hands along Cupcake's trembling spine.

"Stealing is stealing no matter who it's for."

"Yeah, well, what are you doing for her? Nothing."

"I haven't exactly worked it all out yet."

"I got forty-three bucks altogether. Don't you even care about that?"

"Izzy loves her horses."

"She loves Cupcake more."

I stare at the wall. There's a big, empty white square where my Bigfoot poster used to be.

"My poster too?"

"I only got fifty cents for that." She shakes her finger at me. "You should take better care of your stuff. One of the corners was ripped."

"Dakota . . ." I open the door, drag her out, and slam it shut.

*

When Dad drops Izzy off, our mom still isn't home.

"Izzy," I say. "I need to talk to you about something."

Izzy nods and follows me into my room. I close the door.

She scoots onto the bed until her striped-sock legs are dangling over the edge. She fixes me with her big blue eyes.

"This is about Bigfoot," I tell her. "All the Bigfoot stuff is gone."

Izzy looks at the place on my wall where the poster used to be. I go on. "Dakota sold all the stuff to get money for Cupcake to go to the vet."

"Big Foo coming home?" Izzy asks.

I shake my head. "No. But I have something to show you."

I run out to the living room to get the laptop.

Dodge is in the kitchen talking to Crash. "Hot dogs?" Crash suggests.

"Could we have ketchup this time instead of jelly?" Dodge asks.

Dakota sticks her head in the door. "What are you and Izzy doing in there?"

"None of your business."

"We're supposed to be saving Cupcake. Now that I made forty-three dollars, I am going to win the all-county maker fair prize, which is five hundred dollars. I'm going to build an auto-animal-tronic pigeon that picks up trash and puts it in the trash can."

"I can hardly wait. Get out of my room."

"What color should I make it?"

"I don't care. *Get out of my room!*"

"Don't you want to hear my other ideas?"

"No!" I shout.

"Yes," Izzy says.

"I'm going to invent an umbrella that will hover over your head so you don't have to hold it," Dakota tells her.

I close the door in her face and then scoot onto the bed next to Izzy and Dodge. We click on the video of the two-legged bear in the news clip: *Walking Bear in the Neighborhood.*

And there he is, a bear walking like a human. His knees stick out a little when he walks, but otherwise he really is a bear.

"Is he real?" Izzy asks.

"Yep. Something happened to his front paws, so he walks upright."

"Will he come to our house?" Izzy wants to know.

"We don't have a lot of bears around here."

We watch the clip over and over, and every time, we laugh.

I don't tell her about the horses. I can't give her that much bad news all at once.

11

A BED WETTER OR A THIEF?

Tonight is guys' night, which always puts Dakota in a bad mood. She says there are more guys' nights out than girls' nights out. That's not true. There are exactly the same number. But on girls' night Dakota has to share Dad with Izzy. He does other things with them separately, but girls' night is for both of them. Guys' night is just for me.

When Dad knocks, we are all waiting for him. I swing open the door.

Dad pushes the doorbell, which doesn't ring. "Mr. Torpse hasn't fixed this?"

"Mr. Torpse doesn't fix anything," I say.

"I've noticed that," Dad says.

"Daddy." Izzy gets up from where she has been stacking Monopoly money. She gives him a big hug.

Dakota's nose is in a book. She is copying levers and pulleys. She looks at him but doesn't get up.

"Why the long face?" he asks her.

"I'm sad about Cupcake," Dakota tells him. "We need money to take her to the vet—"

"Did you get the kitty litter?" Dad asks.

"Yeah, thanks, Dad, but it didn't help," Dakota says.

Izzy nods. "We need doggy litter," she says.

Dad laughs.

"We've been trying to retrain Cupcake, but I don't think she can control herself. Maybe it's the pills that are making her pee all the time," I say.

Dad jiggles his keys; his eyes are fixed on the stairwell. He does not like doggy bathroom talk. "You ready, Liam?"

"Could you bring us back French fries? Just one order or maybe half of one," Dakota pleads.

Usually we bring them fries, but Dakota knows I'm mad, so I won't remind Dad to get them.

"They're for Izzy too," Dakota wheedles. Then she whispers in Izzy's ear.

"They all for me," Izzy says. "Every one."

In Dad's car, we start talking about tennis, school, and Dodge. I like talking to Dad about stuff. He asks me different kinds of questions than Mom does. And there's only a little insurance stuff. Liability. A favorite topic. It means the person who is responsible for paying the bills if you get hurt . . . or something like that.

Then he turns on a podcast of some guy talking about the power of positivity.

Dad watches a lot of TED talks on how to improve your attitude. I know he's trying hard at his new job, but it worries me. Do other guys' fathers listen to stuff like that?

That's the trouble with being a kid. Nobody ever tells you the right things to worry about.

Then I start thinking about Cupcake again. If Cupcake were a human, nobody would get rid of her because she wet her bed.

I mean, if Cupcake really can't control herself . . . That gives me an idea. "Dad, can we stop at the 7-Eleven?"

"Sure," he says. "But no candy until after dinner."

"Yeah, I know."

At the 7-Eleven, he hands me a ten-dollar bill and I push open the door, my feet sticking to the gummy floor. I step around the potato chip display. There is only one guy, with long blue hair, standing in front of the rotating hot dogs, and an old lady wearing camouflage fatigues behind the counter. I go up and down the aisles, breezing by the candy until I find what I'm looking for . . . diapers. I pick the largest size. I'm just walking to the cash register when the door opens.

It's Moses. And I'm carrying extra-large diapers!

I shove the package under my shirt and hold it there. I'm so busy with this that it takes me a full minute before I realize the kid who just walked in and is now standing by the red slushy machine is not Moses. I've never seen him before in my life.

"Hey!" the old lady at the register shouts, waving her arm in my face. "I saw that. Pay up, kid."

"What? No, I, um, uh, was . . ." My stomach sinks. How am I supposed to explain this?

The old lady clomps out from behind the counter in her big army boots. "I saw what you did. I wasn't born yesterday. I know what you boys do."

My hand shakes as I lift up my shirt and hand her the diapers.

The old lady's head snaps back. Then she peers over her glasses at me. "What else you got in there?"

"Nothing. I swear."

Her eyes narrow to slits. She snatches the diapers and walks around me looking for lumps. When she doesn't find any, she shakes her head. "For goodness' sakes"—she waves the diapers in the air—"why would you steal these?"

"I was going to pay for them. I just didn't want anyone to see." I hand her the money, my face burning like I just played three sets in one-hundred-degree weather.

Her hand closes around the ten-dollar bill, but her face softens. "You got a problem, son?"

Is it worse to have her think I'm a bed wetter or a thief? I don't know.

I'm still shaking when I get back in the car, the diapers safely hidden in a brown bag, which I paid an extra ten cents for. I must look upset, because Dad doesn't ask me for his change. That's lucky, since the diapers were way more expensive than I thought they'd be.

✳

Inside the restaurant Dad lets me order a milkshake.

"I know you're tired of hearing about Cupcake, but we are all really worried about her," I say.

He nods. "I know you are. But life doesn't work out the way we want it to sometimes. Even if we did have the money for UC Davis, there's no guarantee they can fix her problem."

"I know. Dad, how come you and Mom sold the house? If we lived there, Cupcake could stay outside."

Dad's neck muscles strain. His lips pull away from his teeth. "I didn't have the best year last year." He leans his head on his hand. "Your mom and I couldn't swing the mortgage plus the extra expenses of running two households."

"Oh." I take all the napkins out of the dispenser and then put them back in.

"Couldn't you be roommates?"

He shakes his head. "It doesn't work like that."

*

By the time the waitress has brought my cheeseburger and fries, Dad's back to talking about insurance.

"Why doesn't it work like that?" I ask.

"Liability?"

"No. You and Mom."

Dad nods. "How many games in a set?"

"Six is the least. Twelve is the most."

"But you can't play thirteen, right?"

"Right."

"Your mom and I have played twelve games. The set is over. And once it's over, you get off the court."

I nod. Then I ask the question I've been wanting to ask for a long time. I don't plan it, it just pops out. "There's this kid at school who spends half his time with his mom and half with his dad. How come we don't do that?"

Dad stirs his iced tea. "Your mom and I thought that would be tough on you kids, shuttling back and forth like that. Especially for Izzy."

"Oh," I say, my eyes on my plate. I'm thinking about how much I used to like it when my father came home to us every day. He'd take off his regular shoes and put on his flip-flops, and we'd go out on the cul-de-sac. Then I'd skateboard and he'd ride next to me on this old scooter that was too small for him.

Guys' night is great, but it's not the same as seeing him every day.

✳

When I get home, Mom is waiting. She has a funny look on her face, like when somebody stares at Izzy.

Does she know what Dakota did?

"I have to take Cupcake for a walk. She's acting like she ate something she shouldn't have," Mom says.

I nod. "One of Crash's cookies."

"Gonna be a long night." She sighs. Whenever Cupcake has an upset stomach, she wakes Mom up in the middle of the night to let her out.

"You want to join me?"

I put my arm back into my coat sleeve. We don't go far on night walks because the girls are asleep. But you can't talk about Dakota in our apartment. Even when she's asleep she hears everything.

Mom clips Cupcake's leash on. She locks the girls in and we walk up the rickety stairs to the driveway, then past the big brown apartments and onto the street.

Tonight it feels like fall. But the weather around here is weird. Tomorrow it may be summer again. "How did it go with Dad?" Mom asks, buttoning up her sweater.

"Fine," I say. I don't tell her about the diapers. Better get them to work first.

Cupcake stops to smell a patch of weeds. My mom watches me. She waits for more.

"Except . . . I asked him why you guys can't be roommates. Then we could live in our old house."

"You did? And what did he say?"

"That you played twelve games; the set was over. And once it's done, nobody wants to stay on the court."

Mom laughs. She nudges Cupcake to move along. Cupcake trots over to a stick and waits patiently beside it. My mom throws it. She lets go of Cupcake's leash and Cupcake takes off after the stick. Then she prances back with it in her mouth. She's really proud of herself.

"I was young when we got married. I didn't understand who I was or what I wanted. It's sort of like asking you if you want to go back to first grade instead of on to sixth. You'd be taller than all the other kids, the chairs wouldn't fit, and you'd already know everything they were teaching there."

"All my friends would be in a different class," I say.

"That too." She nods.

"Yeah, but you always say family first. Dad is family."

"Yes, and he always will be, but I think you're old enough to understand that relationships are complicated."

"I guess," I whisper.

"I'm sorry, Liam. I wish I had a different answer for you." She pulls on Cupcake's stick, which splits into two. Cupcake tries to fit both halves in her mouth. "So, what happened at the maker fair meeting? Were a lot of parents there?" Her voice has a little squeak.

"Yes."

"Oh boy." She looks up at the small yellow sliver of a moon with the big shadow of a full moon beside it.

"The teacher asked if Dakota had a parent with her. Then Mr. Gupta jumped in because Dakota was driving Mrs. Johnson crazy. But Mr. Gupta is going to help her with her project."

"Mr. Gupta is your tennis coach, isn't he?"

"Uh-huh, and he teaches science to fourth and fifth."

"You like him?"

We circle back to our driveway.

"Yeah. Don't worry, Mom. He knows how to figure kids out."

Mom drops the leash handle so Cupcake won't pull her down the stairs. She holds the handrail and waits at the top while we finish our conversation.

"Did Dakota tell you what else she did?" I ask.

Mom picks at the splintery stairwell banister. "There's more?"

"She sold my Bigfoot stuff and Pinky, Purpley, and Bluey on eBay."

"How is that even possible?" Mom cries. "I curse that laptop."

Uh-oh. She's not going to take the laptop away, is she? She's always saying they didn't have laptops when she was a kid. They had to look up words in a book. "We can't do our homework without it!" I cry.

She nods. "So you say. Does Izzy know?"

"She knows about Bigfoot, but not about Pinky, Purpley, and Bluey."

"Dakota just can't understand that other people see things differently than she does."

"Tell me about it."

"It's because she's young."

"She's in third grade, Mom. I wasn't like that when I was in third grade."

"Every child is different." She sighs. "Look, I really appreciate how good you are with her. I know she can be challenging."

"Mom . . . really . . . what's wrong with her?"

"Nothing's wrong with Dakota. Cunning as a dunny rat, maybe. I mean, I don't even know how she managed to start her own eBay account." She laughs. "But she'll grow into herself. You'll see."

"She did it with your PayPal account. The password comes up automatically on the laptop."

"Oh boy." Mom sighs again.

I follow her down the stairs to where Cupcake is waiting patiently for us. "Izzy's the one who's supposed to be hard."

"It's funny, isn't it?" She smiles at me as she opens the door. "But you do well with both of them. I really appreciate you, love."

Sometimes I like when she says things like this. Other times, I wish she wouldn't depend on me so much.

12

THEY SCARED BY THEMSELVES

In the living room, Izzy is waiting for us in her purple unicorn pajamas.

"Mommy, my horses. Pinky, Purpley, and Bluey are gone. Only the Brownies are here."

Mom flashes a look at me. She unhooks Cupcake's leash, washes her hands, and then gives Izzy a hug. "Let's the three of us sit down. I brought home biscotti."

"Biscotti!" Izzy's face breaks into a grin. Izzy and I sit at the table while my mother turns on the burner under the teakettle. She sets the biscotti on a plate and pours Izzy and me each a glass of milk.

Cupcake starts whining, so Mom lets her onto the patio.

While she's gone, Izzy leans forward, her plastic chair squeaking. "Why are Pinky, Purpley, and Bluey gone? Where did they go?"

"They went to help Cupcake," I say.

"But Cupcake is here," Izzy says.

I MISS IZZY! SHE USED TO BRUSH MY MANE LIKE NO ONE...

OH YES, SUCH A LOVELY LITTLE GIRL! BUT WE DON'T MISS...

CUPCAKE THE LEG NIBBLER!

"Dakota sold them to get money for Cupcake."

"I gave money," Izzy says.

"Monopoly money," I explain.

"Monopoly money is not real," Izzy says. She sits back in her chair. Her feet swing, kicking the table-cloth. "Will Pinky, Purpley, and Bluey come home?"

I shake my head.

Izzy's eyes fill up. "Never?"

"Never," I whisper.

"They scared by themselves."

"They'll talk to each other. I've heard them do it before," I tell her.

Tears run down Izzy's flushed cheeks. "How do they know that?"

"They just do," I say.

Mom comes back now. She sees Izzy crying. "You told her?"

I nod.

The door to Izzy and Dakota's room creaks open. Dakota pads out to us, rubbing her sleepy eyes. "Biscotti," she mumbles, pulling out a chair and dropping into it.

Mom's lips disappear. Her eyes get hard. "We're talking about Pinky, Purpley, and Bluey. I am furious about this, Dakota!"

Dakota's shoulders slump down. "Why?"

"You know why," I snap.

"I'm trying to save Cupcake. Don't you even care?"

"Yes, but you can't take people's things and sell them without asking. Ever. You've got to learn to respect other people's property and their privacy."

"How could I ask them? What if they said no?"

"What if Liam sold your pink kitty?" Mom asks.

"Pink Kitty is missing a paw. Nobody would buy Pink Kitty with only three paws."

"That's not the point. Look, love, your heart is in the right place, but you can't steal."

"It wasn't stealing. You can't steal from your own family."

"Yes it was!" I say.

"But we all want to save Cupcake!"

"Dakota," Mom says, "you know you have to ask permission—"

"You're the one who's giving her away," Dakota interrupts. "You haven't asked *our* permission."

Mom nods.

"I have to save Cupcake *from you*!" Dakota shouts.

"Pinky, Purpley, and Bluey are going to save Cupcake," Izzy says, her voice thick from her stopped-up nose.

"Oh, Izz." Mom folds her in her arms.

"Oh, Izz," Dakota mimics. "She's not trying to save Cupcake. I am."

DOGGY DIAPERS

The next morning when I wake up, I'm still mad at Dakota. My Bigfoot stuff is almost as important to me as Roger Federer. She knows that.

But I need her help making a doggy diaper. Dakota has great ideas, though I will never in a million years tell her that.

I go into Dakota and Izzy's room with my 7-Eleven bag. Izzy is still asleep. Dakota is standing on her bed, feeling along a shelf with her hand.

"What are you doing?"

"Nothing." She yanks her hand back.

I roll my eyes. Then I take the diapers out of the bag and set them on her bed.

"Izzy doesn't need those anymore—ohhhhh!" She hops off the bed. "Do you think they'll work?"

"Worth a try."

"How'd you pay for them?"

"Dad let me make a candy run."

She grins.

I open the diaper package and then call for Cupcake, who is dead asleep by the door. My mom says it makes us safer to have a German shepherd. I guess she's right. Cupcake is a great watchdog, except when she's sleeping. I don't know what she'd do if the bad guys had treats, either. Probably wag her tail.

"Cupcake," I call again. She gets up reluctantly, stretching her back legs behind her. Then she trots to Dakota and Izzy's room.

We close the door so Mom won't see, and I open up one of the diapers. Where will her tail go?

Dakota runs for the scissors and I search the junk drawer for duct tape. I love duct tape. I made a wallet out of duct tape for Father's Day.

A wallet is a lot more complicated than a diaper.

Only, Cupcake won't stand still. She doesn't like when we touch her tail. We duct-tape three diapers together, but it's the wrong shape. We try cutting out places for her legs and a place for her tail. But when we get the thing on, it looks more like a skirt than a diaper.

Dakota takes another diaper and puts one leg

hole around Cupcake's tail and one around her private parts. This kinda-sorta works.

"We just need to get it to stay on. I know!" I run back to the junk drawer for string. Then I cut holes in the diaper, tie string to both ends, and then tie the two strings around her back.

Dakota ducks under Cupcake's legs.

"Uh-oh," she says from underneath. She makes a few adjustments.

In the middle of the procedure, Cupcake lies down with a thump and won't get up.

When she finally stands up, the diaper is hanging off to one side like a wing flap. Cupcake scratches. Then she pulls the diaper off with her teeth and stands at the door whining to be let out.

"What's the dog so upset about?" Mom calls from the living room.

"Nothing," we shout.

"I know," Dakota whispers. "Maybe we can teach her to pee into the toilet."

I run for the doggie treats. Dakota and I squeeze into the tiny bathroom. Together we lift Cupcake onto the toilet, but she slips all around, scrambling wildly.

We try again. This time she yelps, bolts for the door, and scratches to be let out.

I try to lure her with doggy treats. She eyes me warily, pawing harder at the door.

Mom knocks on the other side. "Do not torment the dog."

We crack open the door and Cupcake makes a run for it.

Dakota sighs. "Doesn't she know we're trying to help her?"

"Guess not."

"Let's check online to see what doggy diapers you can buy look like," I suggest.

Dakota gets the laptop and we sit side by side on my bed clicking on "doggy diapers." "They cost more than fifty dollars."

"No!"

"Yeah, because you got to get these liners," I say.

"Here, this one says 'washable.' I guess you wash it out every night," Dakota says.

"We only go to the Laundromat once a week."

"How much would seven cost?"

"Seventy-five dollars or so."

"Are you kidding me? I'm going to invent a disposable doggy diaper and become a millionaire," Dakota announces.

"There already is one. It would cost us around fifteen dollars a week."

"I'll invent a cheap one, then."

"Is that before or after you cure cancer?"

Now Izzy knocks on my door and I open it. She tries to drag Cupcake in, but Cupcake won't come near us and Izzy lets her go.

"I think Cupcake has had enough of this diaper business," I say.

"Cupcake big girl now," Izzy announces. "No diapers."

But when I go into the living room, I see a new yellow puddle by the television.

14

SUPERHEROES DON'T HAVE SISTERS

Monday morning, when I wake up, the rain is drumming on the back patio.

My mother comes in with her umbrella dripping. Cupcake shakes water droplets all over the floor. Mom throws an old beach towel around her and dries her off.

Monday is tennis team, but rain means it will be canceled. There is only one place in our town with inside courts, and you have to be a member. Only rich people can afford that.

Mom doesn't play tennis. She doesn't understand. Luckily, Dad does.

I wish we could have moved to an apartment with a wall I could hit against. Or one of those complexes that have their own tennis court.

The rain makes me grumpy, but I wear shorts and bring my racket—just in case it clears up. I never wear a raincoat. No guy in fifth grade does. Dakota isn't big on raincoats either. Izzy wears rain boots that look like ducks and carries a pink umbrella that matches her raincoat.

We run up the stairs and out to the street, piling into Mom's little red car. She's dropping us off at school today, because she has a meeting with Izzy's teacher and the speech pathologist.

The drops splat on the windshield. *Slap, swish, slap, swish.* The wipers are on high speed as Dakota rattles on about Mr. Gupta. "He does not have ideas on his own and so he has asked me to come up with some. Some adults"—she points to her head—"just don't have it up there."

"Adults are smart," Izzy says. "They take a test."

"An adult test?" I ask.

Mom smiles. "No test, Izzy. But maybe there should be. Not all adults are smart."

"Why?" Izzy asks.

"That's a million-dollar question."

"Mom says that when she doesn't know the answer," Dakota tells her.

"You know?" Izzy asks Dakota.

Dakota stares out the window at the slick side-walk. "Stupid kids grow up to be stupid adults. Nothing to be done about it, unless I discover a cure for stupidity, which I will work on, but not right now."

Mom stares at Dakota in the rearview mirror. "You are on thin ice."

"I didn't mean—"

"Rubbish, Dakota! Listen to me," Mom says. "We are family. One family. One. And we watch out for each other."

"I know, Mom. I'm the one trying to keep us together. I'm the one trying to save Cupcake, remember? It's just that there's only one of me."

"Liam and Izzy have good ideas too."

"Not as good as mine." Dakota crosses her arms.

"Dakota," Mom says.

"Okay, we're a family. But . . . Cupcake is the glue that holds us together, and nobody gets that except me."

✳

When Dakota and I get out of the car, I can't resist asking her: "What happened?"

"I had to close my eBay account. I'm not supposed to go on there ever again, and I have to clean the patio every day for a month and give Pink Kitty to Izzy."

"Pink Kitty! Wow, that is bad." I try not to smile too big.

"But when I win five hundred dollars, everyone will thank me."

✳

Outside class, the two-tone-hair kid is hunched over his phone. Moses has his phone out, but he's nodding to guys he knows. A nod from Moses means a lot.

"Liam." Moses nods to me. "You brought your racket."

"Just in case."

He smiles. "I hope it stops raining. Did you bring the Bigfoot stuff?"

The one thing Moses asks me to do and I blow it. I was hoping he wouldn't remember.

"Forgot?" he asks.

"Uh, well."

"He doesn't really have anything. He was lying, man," the kid with two-tone hair says.

"I'm not lying. My sister, um, sold my stuff," I mumble.

"Why'd she do that?"

I shrug. "Who can explain sisters?"

Moses laughs. "How much she get for it?"

"Not enough," I mutter.

This would never happen to someone like Moses. Moses's family would have enough money to take his dog to the vet. His biggest worry is where to keep the remotes for all his stuff.

"Better lock up your tennis racket," Moses says.

"I know, right?" I try to smile.

But then I look down at my racket. We got it used and we've never even paid to have it restrung. The grip looks shabby because I use it so much. Moses has a Babolat. Brand-new. I know Moses isn't making fun of my racket. But I feel bad anyway.

"Know what my sister did once?" Moses whispers.

I shake my head.

"Held my book report ransom. It was due the next day. She wouldn't give it back until I painted toenails at her slumber party."

"Really?"

He nods. "Seventy toenails and I painted every one."

We all laugh.

"Know why superheroes don't have sisters?" Moses asks.

"Couldn't get anything done," I say. "But some do, don't they?"

Moses shrugs. "Nobody ever asks you if you want a sister, that's for sure."

"Tell me about it," I say.

"Changes your life forever and you aren't even consulted. Listen, you get your Bigfoot stuff back, you keep it at my house, okay, dude?"

He fist-bumps me.

✳ **15** ✳

COUNTING THE DEAD ONES

After dinner I check the laptop for the weather tomorrow. Seventy percent chance of rain. I text Dodge.

Hit w Crash 2moro?

He texts back. *Rain.*

I reply. *Not 4 sure.*

This time he doesn't answer.

✳

Dakota sits on a kitchen stool, her furry pink slippers popping on and off her heels. With her right hand, she's drawing. With her left hand, she's trying to find her mouth with her spoon.

"Nice pictures, Dakota," Mom says.

"They aren't pictures, Kimberly. They're diagrams."

"Diagrams, of course. Silly me." Mom smiles. "And since when did you decide to call me Kimberly?"

"I'm trying it out."

"The name Mom has been around for thousands of years. I think it's a keeper."

"We'll see," Dakota answers.

"Put your bowl in the sink and get ready for bed," Mom says.

"Look, I'm washing my bowl." Izzy turns to Dakota. "I wash out your bowl?"

Dakota nods.

"That's nice of you, Izzy," Mom says.

"I nice," Izzy says.

"*I'm* nice," Mom corrects her. "Come on, nice girl, let's get your teeth brushed."

I take a peek at Dakota's diagrams. I hate to admit it, but I don't know what to do about Cupcake and I'm actually hoping one of Dakota's crazy ideas will work. "How are you going to make the umbrella hover?" I ask her.

"Drones."

"They'll be expensive."

Dakota shrugs. "My other idea is an exploding piñata. That way nobody has to hit it for the candy to come out."

Mom comes into the hall.

She hands Dakota her toothbrush. "No more explosions. Remember our deal?"

"How about quiet ones?"

"No such thing."

Dakota hops to the bathroom, still holding her diagrams. A minute later she bursts out, toothpaste dripping down her cheek. "Mom—I mean, Kimberly. Will you promise not to give Cupcake away until after they award the money?"

"What money?" Mom asks.

"For the maker fair projects. We turn our projects in on Thursday, and then they tell us which will represent our school for all-county, but then it takes three weeks for the county to decide."

"Is that true, Liam?"

I nod.

Dakota glares at me. "Why'd you have to ask *him*?" she says to Mom.

"Just making sure you both heard the same thing."

"The words are the same. How could we hear them differently?"

"It happens." Mom sighs. "Look, we can't wait three weeks."

"You always say I'm smart and I can do whatever I want to. Well, I want to wait three weeks," Dakota declares.

"I know you do, but Torpse gave us three weeks,

and that was almost two weeks ago—" Mom grabs Cupcake just as she's about to pee and hauls her outside.

"Liam will talk to Mr. Torpse about it," Dakota shouts.

I swivel on my heel. "Me? I will?"

"He likes you," Dakota says.

"He doesn't like me. He doesn't like anyone."

"You can make him like you, though. You know you can."

"No I can't."

"Mr. Gupta likes you."

I nod, a warm feeling rolling over me.

"How'd you do that?" she whispers.

I stare at her. Since when does Dakota care what other people think?

"I try to get along with people," I say.

"That's too hard."

"Love"—Mom is back inside with Cupcake now— "we don't know if you'll be picked to represent the school and we don't know you will win the all-county. Let's not count our chickens before they hatch."

"That makes no sense," Dakota says. "Anybody with any brains would count their chickens before they hatch. Otherwise they wouldn't know how many chickens they'd have. And then they'd compare before with after. They'd make two columns.

Dead one. Live one. Dead one. Live one. Wouldn't you make two columns, Kimberly? Wouldn't you?"

Mom and I laugh.

Dakota struts around the plastic chairs and then she gives a big bow.

* 16 *

SKITTLES RULE

When it rains, we have recess in the cafeteria. Mr. Gupta runs rainy-day games, which always involve Skittles. Kids will do anything for Skittles. Skittles rule.

Every once in a while, a parent will complain and then we have to switch to brussels sprouts. But nobody is going to run their fastest for brussels sprouts.

Yesterday we played Skittles relay. Today we're tossing Skittles with our nondominant hands. Mr. Gupta puts the Leadership Council kids in charge. Then he blows a whistle and everybody moves from station to station. Dodge helps me.

I'm getting more caution cones from the back when I see Dakota talking to Mr. Gupta. Dakota is hopping up and down. "I don't see why we can't," she says.

"A hoover umbrella is challenging and will take more than four days—"

"Hover," Dakota corrects.

"Hover, yes. But I do not think you can complete this by Thursday," he says as five kids stampede toward him.

"Mr. Gupta, Jacob got two turns," somebody yells.

"I won. They said I didn't but I did," a kid with orange hair insists.

"But would it still be eligible for the five hundred dollars—would it?" Dakota is hopping again.

"I will talk to Mrs. Johnson about this. Do you have some idea of how you will get your umbrella to hover?"

"How do airplanes fly?" Dakota asks.

"That is a good question, Dakota Rose. But I do not have time for a full explanation at this moment. It has to do with the air pressure on the top of the wing pushing down and the air pressure on the bottom of the wing pushing up."

Dakota chases after Mr. Gupta. "Is it like a leaf blower?"

Why does she do this? Dakota is like a battery-powered ride-on that keeps going and going. Will a teacher stop liking you because your sister is a pain?

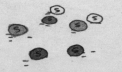

"Mr. Gupta!" another kid shouts. "I won. They said I didn't!"

"Mr. Gupta! Mr. Gupta! Milo's sucking the Skittles then putting them back."

"Dakota, we'll talk again," Mr. Gupta says.

Dakota sighs a big, deep sigh.

✳

At home after school, I'm just pouring myself lemonade when my phone buzzes with a text. It's Moses! Moses is texting me!

Wnt 2 ply sngls tmoro?

He wants to play with me! It's not raining right now, but the sky is dark and heavy and the ground is wet. It's supposed to rain for the next four days. Just my luck.

I text back a rain emoji. Then I look up at Dakota, who asks, "Do we have a leaf blower?"

"No. We don't have any leaves."

"Let's ask Torpse the Corpse."

"He wouldn't even let us borrow the trash in the trash can."

Dakota is looking up into the empty air. "I know!" She thunders out of the room and begins digging in the bathroom drawer. A few minutes later she comes back with a blow-dryer and an umbrella. Then she sits down and begins dismantling the umbrella. Next

time I see her, all the metal parts are in a pile on the floor and she's using the blow-dryer to try to get the sagging fabric to stay up.

My phone buzzes again. Moses!

My club

Of course he has a club. Man, I hate my life.

Not a mber. I stare at my words for a full minute. But I don't see any way around this. I push send.

Dakota tries putting some of the metal ribs back in. They don't stay. Then she gets out the duct tape and cuts cardboard into a big circle.

Then my phone buzzes.

Gust pass

I start jumping up and down. And then it occurs to me that a guest pass will cost money too. I text back.

$$$?

A second later Moses replies: *$0. U my gust*

I'm his guest? *Moses's guest!* How great is that? I get out my tennis ball and start tossing it around. How many guys get to play tennis when it's pouring rain outside?

"What we need are wings," Dakota says. "Or I can discover a new element for the Periodic Table of Elements."

I tune her out. All I can think about is getting to play against Moses. He is good. Really good. But I'm good too.

Will I win? Will he want to play with me again?

I get Cupcake and my tennis balls and go outside. I practice my serve toss, and when I don't catch the ball, Cupcake runs it down for me. We have it all worked out, Cupcake and me.

17

TIEBREAKER

There is a lady behind the desk who is wearing a blue short-sleeved shirt with *Bayside Club* embroidered on it. She looks at me like she knows I'm not a member and she can see that I live in a basement apartment and my mom sleeps in the living room and we don't have enough money to take our dog to the vet.

I hang back.

Moses heads for the counter with long strides.

Moses gives the lady his member number and then hands her a guest pass. She nods, and then she asks me to enter my name, address, and phone number on a tablet. I figure that's in case somebody steals something. They'll know where to look.

I keep one eye on Moses as I'm typing in my address. He won't peek, will he? Nope. He's walking toward a room with a movie-theater-size TV and a blender bar with fruit drinks. There's a basketball court, a pool, and rooms for exercise and yoga classes.

Big windows look out on the indoor tennis courts, where people are playing. The courts aren't the usual green, but blue, and there isn't a single crack in any one of them. The nets are the perfect USTA height, not pulled too tight or sagging too low in the middle. The ball makes a funny sound when it bounces inside the cool, echoing courts. The ceiling is tall enough to lob, so long as the lob isn't crazy high.

Guys with iced drinks watch the tennis players through the big windows. When Moses and I get out there, they'll be watching us. If I'm playing well, I don't feel embarrassed when people watch me play. I kind of like it.

On the courts we put our stuff on a bench next to a water cooler. I look down the row of courts. There's a water cooler on every one!

Moses gets his racket out of a big bag with two rackets inside. My racket sticks out of my backpack, along with a can of used balls. I wonder if they even let you play with used balls here.

When you play with someone who hits hard, they make you look good. If you play with someone who hits sloppy, loopy balls with weird backspin, you don't.

At first my feet stick to the court and my racket slips around in my hand. The ball floats up. A moon ball, really?

My chest tightens. I hope those guys with the drinks aren't watching me now.

But then I forget about everything except Moses's hard topspin balls clipping toward me. I have to stand way behind the baseline to hit them.

Moses and I rally until I find my groove. Now that I'm hitting better, I'm hoping somebody is watching—somebody who will ask me to join Moses's other team. The one he plays on here.

We hit for a long time; then we take a break to guzzle water.

"You want to play or just hit?" Moses asks.

What, is he crazy? Of course I want to play him. "Play."

Moses grins. "Good, because I've been holding back. Being real gentle with you."

"Yeah, right."

He laughs. "Too bad kids in our class aren't here. They'd be rooting for you."

"No they wouldn't."

"Yeah they would, but I'm going to beat you anyway."

We start the real game. Moses serves first. His serve kicks right. The trick is to know the kick is coming and watch the ball extra hard. Moses makes some unforced errors and I win the first game. Then he wins, then I win, then he wins.

My hair is wet with sweat. It's humid in here, and the rain pounds on the canvas roof. I wipe the sweat off my hands. But when we change sides, I see he is sweating too and he doesn't look so confident as he did when we started.

Now we are at 6–6, and I imagine the guys

watching are tennis scouts and they're going to offer to sponsor me and give me my own tennis bag.

We have just decided to play a tiebreaker when, out of the corner of my eye, I notice a man approaching. This is my chance!

But when I turn around I see he has gray hair, cut short, and he's kind of stooped. He's wearing weird black yoga pants, black socks, and Birkenstocks.

Mr. Torpse.

He shakes his crooked finger at me. "I thought I saw you out here."

I can't help but be proud he saw me playing so well. Maybe he'll tell my mom and she'll get me tennis lessons from a pro, like Crash suggested. If your landlord says something, then don't you have to do it?

"Your mother is always telling me she's just scraping by, and here you are."

"I have a guest pass," I mumble.

He snorts. "You tell your mother she has three days to get that dog out of there. Three days. That's it. No one pulls the wool over Melvin Torpse's eyes. No one!" He turns and limps away.

"Yes, sir," I mutter as Moses leaps over the net. "What was that all about? Are we out of time?"

"He didn't say," I mumble.

Moses nods. "Everybody wants to play in here when it rains. They don't cut you any slack. I'll go check." He trots off the court and in the door that leads to the lobby desk.

While he's gone, I think about Torpse's words. Mom said we had a week. Did Torpse move the deadline?

When Moses comes back, he's chewing on the inside of his cheek. "We can play a tiebreaker, but then we have to stop."

Now all I can think about is Cupcake curled up under the table. Cupcake licking the sleep spit off my face. Cupcake shoving her dish around the kitchen when it's time for dinner. Cupcake with her black lips that always look like she just ate licorice. Cupcake loving me with all her big, loyal heart even when I'm in the world's worst mood.

Moses wins the tiebreaker: 7–1.

SCIENCE IS NOT
JUST FOR GIRLS

Moses's sister picks us up. She has hair braided tightly along her scalp and then a ponytail of braids. I move the big stack of schoolbooks on the backseat and sit down.

"You're Liam, right?" she asks.

I nod.

"I'm Jada. Moses's favorite sister." She grins.

Moses rolls his eyes.

"Where do you live?" she asks when we're buckled in.

"Oh, uh, yeah . . . just drop me off at, you know, Camino."

"It's raining. Don't you want me to drive you home?" she asks.

"No, I, um, want to practice my, you know, sprints," I say lamely.

"Okay." She shrugs.

"Your sprints . . . really?" Moses whispers.

"Uh-huh," I say, but I don't meet his eyes. I'm pretty sure he knows I'm lying.

After they drop me off, I watch them turn up Rialto toward the fancy houses with the big lawns with trampolines and riding lawn mowers.

When I pull out my phone, there's a string of texts from Dodge. *D blew up microwave. At my house. Meet there.*

It is raining, so I half run the rest of the way to Dodge's house.

I'm sopping wet when I get there. Dakota is sitting on the front porch with Cupcake. "What did you do?" I ask.

"Nothing."

"How'd the microwave blow up if you did nothing? Mom made you a list of what you aren't supposed to put in there. It's taped to the door."

"I know . . . I've read it a billion times."

"Yeah, so why did you blow the thing up?"

"I didn't put anything in there. Mom didn't put 'nothing' on the list."

"Why'd you run the microwave with nothing inside?"

She juts out her chin. "I thought it might lead to an important discovery. I only have two days until the maker fair projects are due. I have to let my mind run free."

I sigh. "Does Torpse know?"

She shakes her head. "The microwave is Mom's."

"That's good, but couldn't you google putting nothing in the microwave to find out what would happen? Why did you have to do it?"

"Mrs. Johnson says you need to think, not just google answers."

Cupcake's leash is tied to a lawn gnome. She paws her Tupperware water dish, flipping it over.

Then she dives down the porch stairs, pulling the gnome behind her.

She pokes her nose under a hedge and comes out with a sandwich.

I try to get it out of her mouth, but she gulps it down in one bite.

"Oh, great." I untie her leash from the gnome and set it back up where it was.

Dodge sees me and comes out. "How was tennis?" he asks.

"Okay," I say.

"Crash said if it doesn't rain, he'd hit with us tomorrow."

"Excellent," I say as my phone starts vibrating. I look at the text. It's from Mom. *Come home.*

I pull Cupcake away from wet grass she doesn't want to stop sniffing and we head home. Mom is out front sweeping.

Mom's face is dirty and sweaty. Her black pants are covered in dog hair and her ponytail droops.

"Mom, can you come to maker fair day on Thursday?" Dakota is jumping up and down.

"What time?"

"Three."

Mom nods. "I can't wait to see what you've been working on." She smiles. When we walk down the stairs to our apartment, we see the big carpet-cleaning machine is back. "Don't tell Mom Cupcake ate that sandwich," Dakota whispers.

"If I were to, you know, get in trouble before then . . ." Dakota's voice gets small. "Will you still come?"

Mom's eyebrows rise. "I'm knackered, Dakota. Please don't tell me . . ."

Dakota scratches at her neck. "I might have made a teeny mistake."

Mom sighs.

"It was nothing, but then it turned into something," Dakota says. "A big something."

"What is it?"

"I blew up the microwave—but I didn't put anything in it."

Mom frowns. "I saw that. But it was on its last legs, and even so it shouldn't blow up if you run it empty."

Dakota perks up. "I know, right?"

Mom nods. "I'll check it out. Do you want to ask your dad to the maker fair?"

Dakota looks at Mom, and then she looks at me. She shakes her head. "Science is for girls, Kimberly."

"Oh really." Mom grins.

Dakota nods. "You can tell him when I win, though. Then I'll have so much money I can buy a new microwave." She runs into her room and closes the door.

✳ 19 ✳

LICKING TOILET SEATS
AND OTHER PROBLEMS

When I get to the science room, Mom is already sitting in front with Izzy, who gets to miss speech therapy so she can watch Dakota. I'm kind of glad Dakota didn't invite Dad, because I wouldn't know who to sit with. We had that problem last year when our aunt got married. Then Izzy and Dakota sat with Mom and I sat with Dad, but I felt like my left foot was in my right shoe for the entire ceremony. I think kids should write a book about what you're supposed to do in situations like that.

"Liam." Mr. Gupta motions to me. "I need Leadership Council help here now."

I look around. No one from Leadership is here except me.

"I invited Moses," he says.

"You did?"

"Yes. He's new and he doesn't have a lot of friends yet."

I give Mr. Gupta a weird look. He normally knows what's what, but this makes no sense at all. Moses has lots of friends. I just don't want him here. If Dakota is going to do something stupid, I'd like as few fifth graders as possible to see it.

"Would you walk each team up to the front of the class so they can present their findings? Then I will do a little introduction. When each group is finished, you can walk them back to their seats."

He says this as if we're in a big theater with hundreds of people in attendance. But we're in a regular classroom with a handful of parents sitting in too-small seats. Mr. Gupta likes to pretend everything is all fancy and he is the master of ceremonies.

Just as I bring the first group up, Moses arrives. When I get back to my seat, he slips in next to me and Dodge.

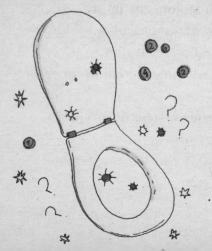

Two boys start with the question: Is it better to lick a toilet seat or lick a coin? They have a poster full of toilet-seat germs and then another one with coin germs drawn in brown and green colored pencil.

They think that most toilets get washed more than most coins, so they conclude it is safer to lick a toilet seat. They have two bottles of hand sanitizer that fit on your belt. One is for your coins. One is for your hands after you touch the coins.

When they are done, Mrs. Johnson jumps up to assure the audience that this is, in fact, a hypothetical question and nobody licked a toilet seat. Mr. Gupta thanks the boys for their questioning minds and for adhering to the scientific process.

Moses escorts the next group up. They have made a Ferris wheel for ants. Then we have a lightbulb inside a cauliflower, and then a bottle opener that fits into your shoe.

Finally, it's Dakota's turn. She is the only team of one. She waits for me, then hops to the front of the class.

Moses laughs. My face gets hot.

"My first idea was a hover umbrella motored by a drone, but unfortunately the money was not there to create the prototip," Dakota announces in an extraloud voice.

Some of the parents laugh.

"Ah, prototype!" says Mr. Gupta. "Good word choice, Dakota."

"So this is just to hold you over until we get the real hover umbrella working."

Dakota dives behind the table. She has constructed

an umbrella out of the large fabric Frisbees the Forty-Sevens use and a metal shish kebab stick attached to a backpack. Dakota pulls out a pitcher and pours water over the Frisbee. The water drips down the sides.

Dakota dances around. "It's a hands-free umbrella. Get it?"

Everybody claps.

Mrs. Johnson grabs a towel and begins mopping up the mess. She looks like she is about to kill Dakota for getting her classroom wet.

Dakota sticks her finger in the air. "Stay tuned. The hover umbrella will be coming soon." Then she comes back and sits with Dodge, Moses, and me.

"Nice job." Moses gives her a fist bump.

Dakota grins.

"I think Mr. Gupta likes me now," she tells me.

✳

When everyone is done, Mrs. Johnson and Mr. Gupta go out into the hall to decide the winner. Then they come back in and announce the maker team who will represent Red Horse Elementary in the county-wide competition. Dakota starts to get up but then drops back down when she hears that the winning team created the Ferris wheel for ants.

"Why do bugs need to go on a carnival ride?" she asks.

I shrug.

Dakota opens her mouth. Uh-oh. She's about to tell Mr. Gupta and Mrs. Johnson they are wrong. But before she can, Mr. Gupta jumps in. "One more winner. In a special category: the most useful idea—which has not yet been implemented to the satisfaction of the committee. And that award goes to Dakota Rose."

Dakota grins at Mom.

Everyone claps and Dakota bows. Then she waves her arm in the air. "Is there money? What about the money?"

Why does she have to say things like this?

"No money, I'm sorry to say, Dakota Rose. But actually there is something far better than money." Mr. Gupta pulls out a bag and sets it on the table.

"Skittles!"

Mom slips her arms around Dakota and gives her a hug. "Great job, love."

Mr. Gupta walks up and offers his hand. "Hello, Mrs. Rose. I'm Mr. Gupta."

Mom shakes his hand. "Nice to meet you, Mr. Gupta. I've heard so many nice things about you."

Mr. Gupta smiles. "I cannot wait for Dakota to be in my science class." He taps his finger to his temple. "Little girl. Big ideas. And I am very much enjoying working with your son. Quite the athlete. The three of them are, actually." He nods toward Dodge and Moses and me.

"Did you hear that?" Dakota asks. "He can't wait for me to be in his class."

"I heard." Mom winks at me.

"Maybe we can sell my idea," Dakota whispers. "Do you think Dad will know how?"

✳

In the car on the way home, drops are running down the windows. Dakota is silent, staring out.

Mom glances back at her.

"Why the sad face?"

"How are we going to make money for Cupcake?"

"We all love Cupcake, but sometimes things happen that are out of our control. And honestly, I wonder if she wouldn't be happier on a farm."

"How could she be happy without us? We're her family."

"We can go and visit her."

Dakota leans forward in her seat. "If I do something you don't like, will you send *me* away?"

"Of course not, Dakota. Dogs are different."

"How do you know? Have you ever been a dog?"

Mom sighs as she waits for the light to turn green.

"What if I started peeing all over the place? Would you make me live on a farm in Sonoma?"

"Don't be so dramatic."

"If it makes you feel any better, I don't think Red Horse is going to win," I say. "I mean . . . a Ferris wheel for ants?"

Dakota nods.

"The Ferris wheel was pretty," Izzy says.

"Yes," Mom agrees.

✳

At home, Dakota follows me into my room and plops on my bed. Ordinarily I would kick her out, but I'm worried about Cupcake too. Mom is sounding more and more serious about giving her away.

"Maybe I could start school somewhere else tomorrow and then I could submit to their maker fair."

"You'd need Mom or Dad to register you in a new school. But we could try doing a bunch of things. And see how much we make. We have two days," I say.

"We have a week," she says.

I shake my head. "No, I ran into Torpse at Moses's club. He said three days and that was yesterday."

"Two days! Did you tell Mom?"

"No. I thought it might make her get rid of Cupcake faster."

Dakota twirls her nerdy wristband. "That was smart."

I don't think Dakota has ever used the word "smart" about anyone but herself before. I smile at her.

"Of course you're smart. You're my brother. And sometimes that one-third nerd kicks in."

I laugh.

"So, what do you think we should do first?" she asks.

"Call everyone we know. See if they can give us little jobs," I suggest.

She nods.

I start with Dodge. When I text him, he says he'll be right over.

Dad agrees to pay us to wash his car. Mom says we can fill gift bags for a bridal luncheon at the restaurant.

When Dodge shows up, he's breathing hard like he ran the whole way. "Crash says we can help him clean out our house."

"Really?"

Dodge leans over, panting. "The magazines and newspapers."

"What are *they*?" Izzy asks as she gallops by with Brownie.

"Newspapers are how people used to find out things before cars but after dinosaurs," Dakota explains.

Mom comes in with a pile of clean laundry, which she sets on my bed. "They still have newspapers, Dakota. They aren't that old. I subscribe now. I read it online."

"That isn't a news*paper,* Mom," Dakota calls out to Mom, who is heading to Dakota and Izzy's room with a stack of folded pink shirts.

"True," Mom calls back, "but it comes from a newspaper company."

"But it's still not paper," Dakota mumbles.

"Whatever, Dakota. Look," I say, "the Forty-Sevens can earn money recycling newspapers." I've been in Dodge's garage. I know how many stacks of newspapers are in there. We'll never get them all cleaned out without help.

"Crash will pay a quarter for every stack. He wants to clean things up so he can have a Sisters in Crime meeting at our house. We got to take them down to the curb before Monday," Dodge says.

"But he's not a sister. Only girls can be sisters," Dakota says.

"They all want to come to the house of a real detective. They treat him like a celebrity," I say.

"How much will we make from that?" Dakota asks.

"A lot," I say.

Dodge nods. "You won't believe how many newspapers there are."

Dakota's eyes glow. "Let's go ask Mom now."

I shake my head. "Let's ask Izzy first."

Izzy is our lucky charm. Mom says yes more often if things are Izzy's idea.

Izzy is sitting on the couch making one of the Brownies leap over the cushions.

"Izzy," I say, "we need your help."

She plunks the horse on her lap with her head in our direction, like she is listening.

I sit down next to Izzy. "We need to ask the Forty-Sevens if they'll help us make money for Cupcake. Will you go with us to ask Mom?"

Izzy gets up and follows us to the kitchen, where Mom is stirring hamburger into the spaghetti sauce.

Mom sighs when she hears about the plan. "You guys, we can't—"

"This is a lot of money, Mom. You have to let us try," I say.

"Try, Mom. Always try," Izzy chimes in.

All of us stare at Izzy.

Mom throws up her hands. "Okay, you win. What day did you want to do this?" she asks Dodge.

"Sunday."

"I'll email them. But don't be surprised if they can't come. Sunday is not our usual meeting day." She looks at Cupcake, who is sleeping on the rug. Two days is all we've got.

"Cupcake, walk!" Mom calls. Cupcake jumps up. This time there's no yellow puddle. Even Cupcake is trying.

* 20 *

BEING CARDBOARD
MUST BE NICE

On Sunday we tiptoe past Torpse's apartment. Yesterday was the deadline for getting rid of Cupcake, but he hasn't said one word about it. Maybe he's forgotten, or changed his mind, or gone back to the old deadline he gave Mom. I try not to think about that right now. We all pile into Mom's car and head for Dodge's house.

Dodge is outside waiting for us. Mom says Dodge and I are in charge. I think Dakota is going to complain, but she doesn't say a word. She's busy poking around, looking at things. We decide to bring the stacks onto the porch and then the Forty-Sevens will carry them from the porch to the curb.

We have more than ten stacks down there when the Forty-Sevens start arriving. Beatrice, with her wild red hair; Emilio, in his button-down shirt; De-Shawn, who somehow ended up with two pink wrist-bands; and Phillipe, in his yellow crocheted cap.

"Your mates are here, Izzy," Mom says with a smile.

"Yay!" Izzy says, and runs out to meet them.

Soon Dodge and I have everyone singing and marching back and forth from the garage to the street.

"We're the herd.
(We're the herd)
Of the nerd.
(Of the nerd.)"

That's when I notice another thing I love about the Forty-Sevens. Compared to them, I am tall. Plus,

none of them would ever embarrass me on purpose the way Dakota does.

The Forty-Sevens are reliable. Nobody takes a break. *Clinkety-clankety*—Crash puts a quarter in the coffee can for every trip from the porch to the curb one of us makes. He paces back and forth, watching the stacks in the house grow smaller.

"You sure this is the right thing to do, Dodge?" Crash asks.

"Your girlfriends need room to sit," Dodge tells him.

Crash rolls his eyes. "They aren't my girlfriends."

Dodge grins.

Crash chews his lip, as he and my mom watch Beatrice carry a short stack of newspapers to the curb. "Lily would have loved the Forty-Sevens." His voice breaks.

"She would have," my mom agrees. "We all miss her, you know that."

"Who do they miss?" Dakota asks.

"Dodge's grandma Lily. She was the one who collected the newspapers."

"How long has she been gone?"

"Four years."

"Four years? How can you miss someone that long?" Dakota asks.

"You can miss someone forever," Mom whispers, squeezing Crash's hand.

Now there are so many newspaper stacks at the curb I give up counting. The coffee can is overflowing with quarters.

"Money." Izzy runs her fingers through the coins.

Crash smiles at Izzy and gives her a hug. "Thanks for bringing your friends over. We couldn't have done this without them."

✳

After we carry the last of the newspapers to the curb, Crash brings out a plate of cookies and a pitcher of punch. The punch is regular. The cookies are peanut butter with bacon in them, but they aren't bad.

Dodge and I walk through the house eating them. "Wow," I say.

Dodge nods. "There's so much more room."

"We can play foosball now," I say. We couldn't play before because there were always stacks of newspapers on the foosball table.

✳

At home, we count the money. Izzy's in charge of putting the quarters into piles of four. I tally the dollar piles. Dakota makes the stick marks. One hundred and twenty-three dollars and seventy-five cents!

"We've got to give some to the Forty-Sevens for helping," I say.

Dakota shakes her head. "I asked them. They said no."

"All of them? Really?"

She nods. "They have our back. And that's a fact."

"I like the Forty-Sevens."

"Me too. But it's not enough," she says.

"Dakota, there's no way we can make three thousand."

"We could sell our mug collection."

"Nobody's going to pay for a bunch of chipped mugs. Besides, Mom said no more eBay."

Mom comes in. She takes one look at our long faces. "Not enough," she says.

We shake our heads. "Nope."

She collapses into my beanbag chair. "At least we gave it a shot."

"There's still time," Dakota says.

Mom nods, but her arms are crossed tight over her belly like she has a stomachache. "I'll tell you what," she says. "Let's sleep on it. Things have a way of looking better in the morning."

In the living room, Dakota curls up on the couch with our ancient laptop. Our laptop is so old that it was created before people had laps.

Izzy starts mumbling about a second person. I think she must be talking about Apples to Apples Junior, a game we like to play. You need a second person to play. I get the box down and open the lid, but my heart isn't in it.

Cupcake comes over and sticks her nose in Dakota's face. Then Izzy sits on Mom's lap.

"What would I do without you all?" Mom runs her hand over Izzy's straight blond hair.

✳

Back in my room, Dakota closes my door. "Liam, let's call Dad."

"I already talked to him. He said he'd pay us ten dollars for washing his car."

"How about if we wash it for the rest of our lives and he pays us five hundred dollars now?"

I dig the phone out of my pocket and press the Dad icon. Dad answers right away. "Hey, Liam. How you doing, buddy?"

"Good. Guess what? We earned a hundred and twenty-three dollars and seventy-five cents toward Cupcake's vet visit. We carried newspapers for recycling."

"A hundred and twenty-three dollars. That's serious money. Good for you."

"But we still need more. We were wondering if, you know, you could help us out?"

"Of course. I'll bring the car over tomorrow."

"Thanks, but could you lend us some money if we wash your car every week forever?"

"Liam." Dad sighs.

"It was worth a try."

"Okay, you gave it a shot."

When I tell Dakota what Dad said, she goes into

her room and lies on the floor next to Izzy's bed so she can hold on to Pink Kitty's tail. I know how she feels.

That night in bed, I stare at cardboard Roger Federer. No matter what happens, he keeps smiling. Being cardboard must be nice.

SOMEBODY INVENTED
UNDERWEAR?

I must have fallen asleep, because when I wake up, Dakota is shaking my arm. "What?" I growl.

"When does the recycling truck come?"

"How should I know?"

"Didn't Dodge say Monday?"

"I think so. What time is it, anyway?" My eyelids do not want to open. They feel like two magnets that don't want to let go.

Dakota flips on my desk light. "Four-fifteen. Liam, look!" She plunks the laptop on my legs.

I try to focus on the screen. "We're not allowed on eBay," I tell her.

"I know, but look anyway!" She points to the top of the screen. *Collectible Newspapers,* it says. *U.S. ATTACKED . . . $19.99; MEN WALK ON MOON . . .*

$49.99; and *MARILYN MONROE DIES . . . $89.99.*

"Who's Marilyn Monroe?" I ask.

"She invented something. Underwear, I think," Dakota mutters.

"Somebody invented underwear?"

"Of course, Liam. You're not born with it."

"Why am I looking at this?"

"Because I saw those papers in one of Crash's piles. They're historical and people want to buy them."

WORLD'S FIRST PAIR OF UNDERWEAR

2 STONES EACH!

5 STONES 60 PEBBLES

"Yeah, but they aren't ours."

"They're nobody's. We put them out for the re-cycling truck."

"We still have to ask."

"Why?"

"Hello, Dakota? It doesn't feel good when people sell your stuff."

"It's not like Bigfoot. Crash is throwing them away."

"Right, but you know how they make you ask permission to use the bathroom? Nobody ever says no you can't do your business, but you still got to ask."

"Okay, okay. But we got to get those papers now before the truck comes or they'll be gone. Didn't Torpse say we only had three more days a while ago?"

"He didn't mean it."

"How do you know?" Dakota asks.

"I don't," I admit.

"Look, they were in a separate stack. Dodge's grandma Lily must have known they were important. I noticed them because the headlines were so big. I woke up and wondered if we could sell them and then I looked and we can!"

It's a good idea. No doubt about it.

"We got to get them now," she went on. "It's the only chance we have."

"We can't go out at night. Mom will—"

"She's asleep."

"Cupcake will bark when we leave."

"We'll take her along."

"We could wake Mom. Maybe she'll drive us."

"On a school night?"

Dakota's dressed already. She's half out the door. If I don't go, she'll go without me.

I pull my clothes on over my pajamas, grab a jacket, and tiptoe to the living room.

Mom sleeps on the sofa. She puts on thick, whitish-green face cream, which makes her look like a zombie.

The dog sleeps in the kitchen. When she sees us, she gets up slowly, stretching her legs. Even she knows it's not morning yet.

I snap on her leash and open the creaking front door. Dakota scoots after me.

Outside it's pitch-black. Torpse is too cheap to fix the lights.

We wait for a second, listening for Mom. But no Mom. She would have been out here already if she'd heard us, so that's good, but we should have brought a flashlight. I try using my phone, only it doesn't put

out much light. I don't dare go back. It's a miracle Mom didn't wake up as it is.

The only good thing about being out at four in the morning is I won't run into Moses.

But it's so dark out here. There are no street-lights and it's too foggy for moonlight. Dakota grabs my hand and holds it tightly. I let her because no one I know will see. We creep by the dark windows of parked cars that look like maybe someone is inside.

In her other hand, Dakota clutches the page with the list of valuable newspapers she wrote out from eBay.

We half run. Most of the apartment windows are dark. Some are dimly lit, but one has all the lights on, and we can hear music blasting. A strange man

stands out front. He has his back to us, like he's hiding something.

I'm glad we have Cupcake along. Cupcake will protect us. But Cupcake pays no attention to the man. She has found a pinecone on the road.

The man sees us.

We bolt forward, running helter-skelter. Cupcake runs with the pinecone in her mouth. I keep looking back for the man but I can't see him anymore.

When we get to Dodge's, we are panting hard. I take off my jacket. Too hot.

I consider texting Dodge. It seems weird to be in his front yard, digging through his newspapers, without him. But it isn't even light out. I text him anyway.

We r in yr yard.

Dodge doesn't come out. He sleeps like he eats. Big and heavy.

Dakota goes straight for a stack of newspapers near the neighbor's driveway. "This one," she says.

But it's too dark to see.

Uh-oh. Dakota and I look at each other.

"Wait," I say. "I know where they have a flashlight." Crash likes to be prepared in case of earthquakes. He keeps their emergency kit in an old metal box under the porch swing.

I sneak up the steps and get it out.

We take turns. One of us holds the flashlight, while the other looks through the pile. At first I hold on to Cupcake's leash, but she keeps yanking on it, so I tie her to an upside-down lawn chair in a corner of Dodge's yard, and she curls up. It's still so early we can hear individual cars roar by on the freeway up above, but not the steady stream we're used to.

We go through the entire stack. Paper by paper. But we don't find a single valuable one.

"They were here. Somebody messed them up," Dakota says.

"Everybody put things everywhere," I say.

"Maybe it's this one." She taps another stack.

We start on that stack, and then another and another.

The freeway sounds are getting louder, and the sky is gradually becoming lighter.

We can see without the flashlight, so we each take a stack.

"Mom will be up soon. We got to get home."

"Just look for the large headlines," she mumbles.

"What do you think I've been doing? You said you knew where they were."

"They got moved. Keep your eye out for 'Marilyn Monroe Dies.' That one is worth the most."

I start on another stack.

She looks up. "Do you think they're in the recycling bin?" She flaps back the lid, which smells of boiled broccoli. When I turn around again, she's climbed into the bin and has half the newspapers out.

"Wait!" Her voice, from inside the container, sounds faraway. Her head pops up. She waves a paper over her head. *"'Men Walk on Moon,'"* she cries.

"How much was that worth?"

"Forty-nine ninety-nine."

Are they all worth that much? I stick the newspaper under my arm.

Dakota dives down again. "Look! Here's *'U.S. Attacked.'"* She pops up again.

"We need *'Kennedy Assassinated'* or *'Marilyn Monroe Dies.'* *'Marilyn Monroe Dies'* is harder. It wasn't a big headline," she says.

The sun is rising: a bright orange ball halfway up the sky.

"We have to go!" I say.

"It's almost a hundred dollars." Dakota's head disappears inside the bin. There's a loud rumbling from the freeway above. Cupcake starts barking. She rushes into the street, pulling the lawn chair. I  chase after her. Then I see that the truck isn't on the freeway. It's coming down the street, lights blinking. There's a *chuff* and a hiss, then loud idling.

RECYCLING, the sign on the truck says.

I run faster, catching hold of Cupcake and the lawn chair and dragging them both back. "Dakota, get out of there!" I shout, but the freeway is so loud, she can't hear.

"Dakota!"

I hear her muffled voice. "I think I got it."

"DAKOTA! DAKOTA!" I shout as the big metal mechanical arms lift the blue bin she's inside.

"OH NO! STOP! STOP!" I wave wildly to the driver, a big guy moving his head to a song's beat.

Cupcake is twisting around, barking in every direction. I hammer my fist against the window. The driver finally sees me.

"Whhhaa?" He pulls a lever that stops the metal arm.

Dakota's bin hovers in the air.

"MY SISTER IS IN THE RECYCLING BIN!" I yell.

WOOF!
WOOF!

He pulls his earbuds out, jumps down from the cab, and walks to the back.

"Can you get me out?" Dakota's voice is small and scared.

"You people," he mutters, climbing up the side of the truck and reversing the arm. He brings the bin back down to the ground with a lurching jolt.

Then he hurries back to us. "I'm gonna lift you out," he tells Dakota.

"I got to hold on to Marilyn," Dakota says.

"Who?" He looks back at me. "Somebody else in there?"

"No," I say. "Marilyn is in the newspaper."

"She's dead," Dakota explains.

The driver shakes his head. "I knew this was going to be a bad morning. Didn't I, Mama?" He taps his truck. Then he lifts Dakota out of the bin and gently places her down. "You okay, little girl?"

Dakota nods. She's got little curds of cottage cheese clinging to her hair. Her face is filthy with newspaper ink. She's holding the newspaper in her hand.

"I got it!" She grins. "But who's Mama?"

"She my truck," the recycling man says.

"I'm sorry, Mama." Dakota pats the side of the green truck.

"Okay." The man smiles at Dakota and pats her head. Then he turns to me. "Take her home, get her cleaned up. She is a sight."

Dakota beams through the white cottage cheese speckles and baked beans hanging from her hair. Cupcake sniffs her shoes.

"C'mon, we got to go," I say.

Cupcake has been quiet, but when I untie her and we take off, she starts barking again and pulling me along. Dakota has both arms hugging the newspapers against her chest.

When we get to our apartment building, we tromp down the stairs and turn the knob as quietly as possible. But as soon as the door swings open, Mom and Izzy are there with their coats on. Mom's purse is over her shoulder; Izzy is holding Mom's hand.

"Oh, thank God you're all right." Mom's voice trembles.

We nod.

"Where were you?" she whispers.

The look on Mom's face makes me feel terrible. We scared her half to death.

"What happened?" she asks us.

"Mommy, Dakota smells." Izzy uses her fingers to close off her nostrils. Dakota is making our apartment smell like spoiled food.

Dakota gives me a sideways glance. "I got kind of dirty, but we got the papers. We got more money for Cupcake."

"I don't know what you're talking about and frankly I don't care. You are not under any circumstance to leave this apartment after dark without me, ever. EVER!"

"But we got valuable papers we can sell! The money—" Dakota squeaks.

Mom puts her hands over her ears. "I don't want to hear one more word about that money."

Dakota's mouth clamps shut.

"And you . . ." She turns to me. "You know better."

"But, but I found newspapers worth a lot," Dakota says. "They are famous."

I nod. "Dakota figured out some of the newspapers are valuable. The ones on the days of important history."

"You are not to put yourself in dangerous situations for any reason. ANY REASON! Do you understand?"

We nod. Better not to argue with Mom when she's this upset.

"Dakota, you have simply got to learn to follow instructions."

"I do follow instructions. *My* instructions."

"That's not what I mean and you know it! Say this will never happen again. Both of you. Say you will never go out alone at night."

"This will never happen again," we both say.

"And?"

"And we will never go out alone at night."

Our mom stares at Dakota, then at me. "Do you have any idea how worried I was? Anything could happen out there in the middle of the night. Why would you want to put me through this?"

"We didn't think you'd know," I offer, but as soon as the words come out I know this was a stupid thing to say.

"Rubbish! Just rubbish!" she shouts.

I hang my head.

"Take showers. Both of you. We'll talk more about this after school."

✳ 22 ✳

THE SECOND PERSON

Mom grounds us for a whole week, which doesn't bother Dakota but about kills me. The weather is sunny and my team holds practice without me!

When we ask Mom about Torpse's deadline, she says she'll go talk to him. But every time she knocks on the door, there's no answer.

Mom lets us sell the historic newspapers on eBay, so it could be worse. And then, when Crash is supposed to watch us, he takes us to the park with the tennis court, so I get to play a little bit. At school Mr. Gupta asks me why I had to miss and I have to tell him. What else could I do?

He listens closely to the entire story. Then he nods and says, "Landlord problems are a lot for a fifth grader to deal with. I am sorry, Liam. Do you think you can make next practice?"

"Yes, sir," I say.

"Good." He smiles.

✳

But today it's raining again, so no practice. Just my luck.

It's a week and a half after the day Torpse said we had to get rid of Cupcake, and he hasn't said one word about it. He must have been bluffing.

Now we have $327.93, which isn't enough for UC Davis, but it might be enough to get Mom's attention. She can't give Cupcake away if we earned this much money . . . can she?

We're discussing the money when Izzy starts talking about a second person again. "I'm tired of Apples to Apples," I say. "Couldn't we play something else?"

Izzy looks confused.

"Go get one of the Brownies," I tell her.

She gets her brown horse and I get some old tennis balls and we go up on to the driveway. Izzy sets her horse up to watch me practice my serve toss. And then she chases the balls down for me and sets them in a neat line for me to throw again. When there are no balls to chase, she works on tying her

shoelaces. She has it now, and she keeps practicing so she won't forget.

After a while, Dakota comes out to join us. "I wonder how long it will take for a big company to buy my hover umbrella," she says.

"You haven't even designed it yet."

"I know. But Mr. Gupta will help. He says I should think hard about machines that hover."

"Like what . . . a helicopter?"

She nods.

"Helicopters are even more expensive than drones. But it would be awesome to have a helicopter hovering over you everywhere you go," I say.

She nods. "I was wondering if you are a flying bug in a car and the car is moving forward, will you move forward with the car or be slammed back. Because maybe there could be—"

"Second person. Second person. Second person," Izzy says.

"Izzy, I'm trying to think of something," Dakota says.

"Second person!" Izzy takes a deep breath and gets up in my face. "Mommy and I go to the doctor and the doctor say one thing." She counts on her fingers. "Mommy says second person."

"Yeah, so?" Dakota says.

"No, wait." I put my hand up. "What do you mean, Izzy?"

"When doctor say one thing, Mommy say second doctor."

"Oh," I gasp. "A second opinion. Izzy wants us to get a second opinion for Cupcake."

Izzy's face relaxes.

Dakota's head pops up. "Another vet's opinion. We have the money for that. Izzy, that's brilliant!"

"Second person." Izzy and I high-five, her face glowing like it has ten lightbulbs inside.

THAT'S MY IZZY GIRL!

23

A NERD OR A GREEK?

After school Mom and Cupcake are supposed to pick us up and take us to Cupcake's vet appointment.

We wait in the car line for Mom's little red car. Instead, Dad's blue car roars up. Dad's car is loud because he needs a new muffler.

Dad cranks down his window. Cupcake is in the car on top of the cardboard that covers the broken seat. Dad's car is clean because Dakota and Izzy and I washed it last weekend.

I like Dad's car because it's old, so no airbags, which means I get to sit in the front.

"I got dibs on the front on the way back," Dakota says as she and Izzy pile in.

"Is Mom okay?" I ask as I buckle in.

"She's fine. She had to work. Two waitresses called in sick. I'm helping her out," Dad says.

"Do you know we have Cupcake's vet appointment today?" I ask.

"Why do you think I brought the dog?"

Dakota nods. "What about the pee samples. Did you bring them?"

"Say what?"

"The pee samples. The vet is going to need them. I have *before* Cupcake got sick and *after*."

"Your mother didn't say anything about that. Did the vet request these samples?" Dad asks.

"It's a new vet. She doesn't know she needs them yet," Dakota says.

"Ahh," Dad says. "Don't you think we better let the veterinarian do her job? That's what you're paying her for, Dakota."

Dakota leans forward. "It's important. We won't get another chance."

"It's way out of our way, honey."

Dakota scowls. She wraps her arms tightly around herself. Then she perks up again. "Did you hear how we made the money for this?"

"Your mom told me all about it. Look, give us a minute, Dakota. Liam is eager to hear about the latest changes to insurance policy."

I peek over, hoping he's being sarcastic.

He isn't.

But he can't get a word in because Dakota is telling him all about how we made money. Then she waits for him to say how brilliant she is.

He looks over at me. "Mr. Torpse said you couldn't have a dog."

"Unless she stops peeing in the house," Dakota jumps in.

"I've got a buddy who has ten acres up in Sonoma. Cupcake could have her run of the place. And you three could spend all that money you made on a new TV."

"No!" Dakota shouts. "Mom said we had another chance!"

I try to stay calm. Dad likes it better when we don't shout.

Dad keeps going. "I know Liam wants a new

tennis racket. And there's probably something you and Izzy want."

"No he doesn't," Dakota butts in.

I think about a new racket. Would I have won that tiebreaker with Moses if I'd had a better racket?

Then I try to imagine Cupcake running free on a farm. No. She loves us. She wants to be with us all the time. She wouldn't be happy without us, and we would be miserable without her.

No one to greet us when we get home. No one to pet when things go wrong. No thank-you visits after we feed her. No morning wake-up nose in our faces. It's bad enough not living with Dad, but not having a dog . . . That is just too sad.

"Mom said we could take her to the vet," I say.

Dad nods. "I know, Liam. I've got the dog and your bag of money. I'm just presenting another alternative here."

✳

When we get to the vet, we all pile out of the car. Dakota snatches the money bag, and we head for the waiting room. Then the veterinarian's assistant, who has dogs tattooed on both arms, lets us into a room with a metal table and glass jars full of dog biscuits. When Dr. Judy comes in, Dakota starts talking right in her face, so close that a drop of spit flies onto the vet's glasses.

"I took her samples before and after she became incontinent. I have Cupcake's pee marked *before* and Cupcake's pee marked *after*. But Dad wouldn't let me bring them. Will you charge extra if we have to come again?"

The vet takes a step back. She takes off her glasses and cleans them.

"What's inconanent?" Izzy asks.

"It means when Cupcake pees everywhere," I explain.

"A cupcake made of pee. Yucky," she says.

Dakota doesn't even hear this, she's so intent on the vet. "I did not know exactly what to test," she says, "but I observed differences. *Before* was slightly cloudy. *After* was clearer."

Dr. Judy raises her eyebrows at Dad and then turns back to Dakota. "I like the way you're approaching the problem. But there are a lot of factors that may have come into play here. Were the jars clean? How old are the samples? Was she fed the same thing on both days? Then, too, if she's drinking a lot of water, her urine is likely to be clearer."

Dakota nods, taking this in.

"Actually . . ." The vet opens the manila folder labeled *Cupcake Rose* and runs her finger down

the notes. "Your previous vet sent her records. The medicine Cupcake was on has significant side effects. Increased urination is one of them."

Dakota and I look at each other. "That's what we thought," I say.

"Have you noticed her panting more than usual?" We nod.

"There's another medication, which doesn't have those side effects."

"Why'd they give her medicine that makes her pee all the time?" Dakota asks.

"Not every dog experiences this. And not everybody knows about the new meds. Besides, the old medicine is cheaper than the alternative, so we generally recommend it first."

"How much more expensive is the new one?" I ask.

"It costs ninety-eight dollars," she says. "For six months. Till her digestion stabilizes."

"And today's visit is?" Dad asks.

"One hundred dollars."

"We have enough!" Dakota swings the big plastic bag of quarters and dollar bills in Dad's face.

"I don't think we've ever received payment in quarters

before. Quite the kids you have," Dr. Judy whispers
to my father.

Dad laughs. "Don't I know it."

✳

Cupcake is curled up in the back, stinking up the
car we just washed. Dakota is so excited she forgets
she had dibs on the front seat. Dad drives us to the
special doggy pharmacy. Dakota counts out more
quarters and Dad goes in to get the medicine.

"Dakota?" Izzy asks. "Am I smart enough to be
a nerd?"

Dakota rolls the window down and I take a deep
breath of fresh, non-doggy-smelling air.

Dakota reaches over to touch Cupcake. "You get
automatic membership because you're my sister."

"Me." Izzy pats her chest. "Am *I* a nerd?"

Dakota takes a deep breath. Her eyes flash on mine.
"We wouldn't even be here without you, Izzy. You're the
one who said we should get a second opinion."

"I did?"

"You did."

I nod. "She's definitely a full member."

Izzy grins. "What about Dad?"

"Dad?" Dakota asks.

"He a nerd or a Greek?"

"Am I a what or a what?" Dad looks in the window. He has the medicine and a bowl of water.

"I don't think we know for sure yet," Dakota says.

Cupcake gets out to take her medicine. As the dog laps up water, Izzy says, "I hope." She uses her left hand to cross the fingers of her right hand. Then she holds her crossed fingers in the air.

"What did she say?" Dad asks me.

"We need French fries."

Dakota laughs as Cupcake scrambles back into the car.

I think Dad's going to ignore me, but a few minutes later he pulls up to the burger drive-through.

"French fries!" Dakota and Izzy yell.

"Didn't get a chance to cook today." He winks at me.

* 24 *

DAUGHTER OF THE CORPSE

We are each gripping a burger bag and a drink when we turn onto our street. Dad stomps on the brakes to avoid the traffic. There are so many apartments on Las Flores that the street gets congested. My phone buzzes with a text from Dodge. *Walkin to ur house.*

I text back. *Gd.*

There are people in yellow vests doing street work, a furniture delivery truck trying to maneuver around some orange cones, and a lot of cars stuck waiting. "Mind if I drop you here?" Dad asks. "I don't want to get caught in that mess."

Dad pulls over and we pile out. Dakota holds the medicine. I grab Cupcake's leash.

"See you next week." Dad waves.

"Bye, Dad! Bye!" we call as he drives away.

We're at the top of the hill when I spot Moses.

I do a double take, hoping I'm wrong. But this time it really is him. I look around for a place to hide. There's a stairway up ahead. If only we can get there. "C'mon," I say.

"Hey, Moses! Moses!" Dakota waves.

Moses turns. "Liam!"

My face feels sweaty, my stomach queasy.

Moses trots back to us. "Hey."

I wish I could dissolve into liquid and pour down the storm drain.

"Moses! You remember me, right?" Dakota hops up to him.

"How could I forget you?" His deep dimples show in his cheeks.

"I'm Izzy." Izzy wraps her arms around his waist and gives him a hug.

Moses smiles.

But I can't smile. I can't even look at him. All I can think about is how I don't want Moses to see where I live.

"Hey, Liam, glad to see you. It's boring at my aunt's place—a bunch of ladies talking about porcelain nails and hair extensions."

"Where does your aunt live?" I ask.

"Four blocks up, at Miranda."

Out of the corner of my eye, I see that our apartment building's driveway is loaded with furniture and boxes.

Moses sees it too. "Somebody must be moving."

"Liam!" Dakota's voice is small. Not the way she usually shouts for the entire world to hear. She grabs my hand.

It dawns on me slowly like I'm in a video game or somebody else's movie. Our scuffed plastic chairs. Our wobbly, cockeyed side table. Our plastic bins with Dakota's scribbling on the back; Dakota and Izzy's pink lamp; Pink Kitty tossed on the ground and Roger Federer bent in two.

My throat closes up. My heart stops beating.

Izzy chatters about her chicken tenders.

But all I can think of is Moses. Why does he have
to be here?

My eyes are fixed on cardboard Roger like I still
can't get it in my head what is actually happening.

And then I know what I'll do. I'll just keep going—
pretend I live somewhere else. I'll take off, say I'm
practicing my sprints, like Mr. Gupta told us to do.

But then in a flash I see myself trying to explain
to Mom how I left Dakota and Izzy on the street with
all our stuff. How I was too embarrassed to stand up
for them and for myself.

"You take Cupcake." I hand Cupcake's leash to
Dakota and race to the driveway. From his porch,
Mr. Torpse is directing a hulking teenager in tight

red jeans with a copy of *Romeo and Juliet* in his back pocket.

"Hey, Gramps. Got a friend going to be here in a few minutes to help us with the beds and bureaus," the teenager tells Mr. Torpse.

"What's going on, Mr. Torpse, sir?" I ask, my voice wobbling.

He turns to me, his bony gray chin stuck in the air. "Your mother has broken the lease agreement."

"She's what?"

He taps his cane on the porch. "Item number twenty-three. No pets."

"But you knew we had a dog," I say.

"Yes, but I didn't know you had a cat."

"We don't have a cat."

"I saw the kitty-litter box."

"That was for the dog."

His squinty eyes get squintier. "That is a lie, young man."

"No."

"In any case, your dog is ruining the carpets."

"Not anymore. The vet gave her new pills."

"A little late for that."

"My mom will pay for the carpets," I say, my heart beating so loudly in my head I can barely hear anything else.

"No telling what other damage that dog and your cat have caused." Torpse turns to Moses. "You look like a nice young man. Are your parents interested in a rental? Got a ground-floor unit, number 2B, available as of today."

"No, sir," Moses mumbles.

"You do not have number 2B available," Dakota says. "That's ours."

"Not anymore, young lady." Torpse cracks his cane on the porch railing.

Moses looks at me. He takes in the situation. "Tell him my mom is an attorney. Tell him you'll sue," Moses says under his breath.

Now Dodge appears by my side. Dodge, who never says anything, opens his mouth. "That apartment is dangerous, sir," he tells Mr. Torpse.

"The stairs are rotted and too steep." I pick up where Dodge left off. "The toilet won't flush unless you take the lid off and attach the chain to the lever every time." I'm on a roll now. "The hinges have broken off the cupboard doors. The refrigerator door fell off on Dakota's foot. The outside lights don't work. We trip on the stairs at night."

Torpse looks away. "That's not your concern anymore. You no longer live here."

Moses nods to me.

"Our attorney thinks it is," I say.

"Your attorney? Well, I'm entirely within my legal rights. I had to call the police just the other day because that one"—he shakes his cane at Dakota—"tried to blow up my stairwell. And that dog there"—he waves wildly in Cupcake's direction—"can't hold her liquids. Spots all over my carpet. And this one here"—he points at Izzy—"sings at all hours. I won't have it." He bangs his cane on a rolled-up yoga mat.

"Yeah, and two of the burners don't turn on." Dakota's hands are on her hips. "My dad says you're supposed to fix things."

Out of the corner of my eye, I see a lady in a bright blue dress and high heels huffing up the hill toward us.

"What's his name?" Moses whispers.

"Mr. Torpse," I hiss.

"My mother is the Roses' attorney, Mr. Torpse," Moses says. "Maybe we should call her."

"This is my attorney, Mrs. Ortega." He points his cane at the lady in the blue dress. "And she is already here."

Mrs. Ortega rolls her eyes. "Really, Dad?"

"My father says that there is a, uh"—what is it Dad's always saying?—"lia . . . liability problem because you don't fix anything," I say.

Mrs. Ortega looks around at our stuff. "Dad, you know I can't represent you. What is this all about?"

"I'm evicting the Roses. The carpet is ruined."

"You got a security deposit. When they move out you can use it for new carpets," Torpse's daughter says.

"They have a cat and a dog that relieves himself on my carpets. They nearly blew up my stairwell." Mr. Torpse's face is bright red.

"Why are you stirring up trouble? They're just kids, Dad. We had a dog when we were kids. Don't you remember Tammy?"

"You don't live here. You don't know," Torpse tells her.

Mrs. Ortega stares at Izzy. "Isn't that the little girl who found my scarf? It is! This is a nice family, Dad."

"I have to protect my investments," Torpse announces.

"I have had it up to here"—Mrs. Ortega puts her hand to her forehead—"with you and your investments. Marco, honey"—she motions to the big teenager in the red jeans—"put their belongings back. And, Dad, you need to apologize to this family right here, right now."

Mr. Torpse stamps his feet. "Marco, you do what I say. *I'm* paying you."

"I don't know, Gramps. She's my mother." Marco moves his thumb in the direction of Mrs. Ortega. He picks up our lamp and heads down the stairs.

"Come on, Dad," Mrs. Ortega says. "Apologize. We're all waiting."

Mr. Torpse's lips are clamped closed.

"I know how you feel," Dakota tells him. "I never want to apologize either. But Mom says you got to do it, even if you don't mean it."

Mrs. Ortega is staring hard at Torpse. "What is the name of that yoga teacher you like so much? Misty. What if I were to tell Misty that you evicted this nice family because *they had a dog*."

"They have a dog and they like to sing and—" He looks over at us.

"Do extra credit," Dakota finishes for him.

Mrs. Ortega's hands fly to her hips. "Extra credit. How could you have a problem with that, Dad? I expect you to say you're sorry, or believe me, Misty is going to hear about this."

Mr. Torpse huffs and puffs. His face is so screwed up it looks like a sponge after it's been twisted to get the water out. He stares hard at his daughter. "I may have made an error. But I may not have."

Mrs. Ortega crosses her arms. "No, Dad. No. Do they pay their rent on time?"

"Always," he mumbles.

"Well, then this is their home and I expect you to apologize right now. I'm not about to make you apple crumble if you act like this."

Mr. Torpse scowls.

"Sometimes I apologize and then I mean it later," Dakota offers. "But your people are your people, Mr. Torpse. They are more important than anyone else."

Torpse sighs, the air bursting out of him. "I'm sorry, Roses," he mutters.

"I'm sorry too." Mrs. Ortega's lively dark eyes fix on us. "Please forgive my father. I don't know what has gotten into him lately. My son will put everything back just as it was. And"—she lowers her voice—"I will work on getting Dad to spring for the repairs."

Mr. Torpse's head jerks up. "What? What did you say?"

"Nothing, Dad." Mrs. Ortega winks at us.

Mr. Torpse's shoulders slide down. But he doesn't say a word as Marco, Mrs. Ortega, Dodge, Moses, Dakota, Izzy, and I carry everything back down. Luckily, none of the really heavy furniture, like our dressers or beds, was moved yet.

Moses sets my Xbox on my bed. "I liked that liability bit," he says.

I still can't look him straight in the eye. This is the worst thing that has ever happened to me. But I am aching with relief that we are back inside. This stupid apartment looks like the most incredible place in the entire world right now, because it's our home.

I take a deep breath and keep myself together. "Hey, is your mom really an attorney?"

"She's a software engineer. Works at Google. Both my parents do. They're total nerds."

"One hundred percent?" Dakota calls from the hall.

He nods. "Yep. Hey, you know what? This is way

better than sitting around at my aunt's. Can I come over again?" His eyes are guarded.

"Sure," I say.

He smiles at me and then at Dodge. "I didn't know if you guys . . . You always do everything, you know, together."

I stare at him.

Moses is the new guy. He was trying to make friends. All this time I've been worried about what he thinks of me. And he's been worried about what I think of him. How could I have gotten that so wrong?

✳

When Mom gets home from work, she asks, "How did everything go today?"

I can see Dakota take a big breath, ready to tell the whole story. I shake my head and she slaps her hand over her mouth.

My mom looks at her, then at me.

"Good," I jump in. "Cupcake has new medicine. The new vet doesn't think she's going to pee in the house anymore."

Mom's mouth drops open. "Really?"

"Yup." I nod, and then Dakota and Izzy nod. Izzy's smile stretches big as our whole street.

"Everything go okay with Dad?" Mom asks.

"He a nerd or a Greek. We wait and see," Izzy tells her.

My mother laughs.

Then she brushes the dog hair off her pants. "I better go up and talk to Mr. Torpse."

"We did that already, Mom," Dakota says.

Mom's eyes waver.

"Dakota's right. All taken care of." I wipe my hands one against the other.

She squints at me, then surveys the living room. "Did you move things around in here?"

Dakota, Izzy, and I look at each other.

"A little," I admit.

"And Torpse might do our repairs," Dakota says. "His daughter said so. She likes Izzy."

Mom's eyebrows rise.

"Might," I say. "You know, maybe."

Mom nods. "For a minute there, I was thinking we were living in an alternate universe."

"What's that?" Dakota asks.

"It's a place like our universe only slightly different," Mom says.

"I bet they have hover umbrellas there," Dakota says.

"I bet they do," Mom agrees. "Did I tell you what a gobsmacking idea that is, Dakota Rose?"

Dakota smiles. "You can tell me again."

Mom laughs. "I can't wait to see what you'll do when you grow into yourself."

"Did you hear that?" Dakota trumpets.

"You do have good ideas, Dakota," I say.

Dakota smiles big as the moon.

"Know what I was thinking, Liam?" Dakota asks. "You know how you're always saying one-third nerd is the right amount?"

"Yeah."

"You, Izzy, and me—our family is one-third nerd."

"You're the nerd?"

Dakota nods. "Yeah, and you're the sports guy and Izzy's the friend-getter."

I waggle my head. "You're kinda right about that,

but your percentages are off. I'm one-third nerd, so all together it's more like four-ninths nerd."

"Don't be so technical," she says.

I cough, practically choking on my own spit. "Wow, Dakota. Maybe there's hope for you yet."

Mom sits down at the table. Cupcake makes a beeline for her. Mom massages Cupcake's ear. "I'd say we had a good day," she says. Then she notices Roger Federer bent over. "Uh-oh. What happened to Roger?"

"He sweated a little today," I admit.

"I see that. Well, it's about time." Mom opens the box of pizza she brought home from work.

I unfold Roger, get out the Scotch tape, and tape the part where he got torn. "I'm gonna put him back." I carry him to my room and set him up just like before.

"Good," Mom calls, setting a bowl of carrots on the table. "I'd miss him if he were gone."

"Yeah," I say. "Me too."

ACKNOWLEDGMENTS

I would like to thank Martha Hogan, Julie Durbin, Kristi DeBisschop, Nico DeBisschop, Maddy DeBisschop, Karen Herz, Griffin Herz, and the Down Syndrome Center of the Bay Area for helping me to understand more about Down syndrome.

A special thanks to Églantine Ceulemans for capturing the spirit of Liam, Dakota, and Izzy with her deft hand and sly humor. And to Leslie Mechanic, who found the perfect illustrator for this book.

Thank you to Sylvia Al-Mateen, Elizabeth Harding, and Sarah Gerton for insightful comments on the manuscript. And to Alison Kolani, Colleen Fellingham, and Janet Fletcher, my copyediting team, who keep me from making a fool of myself. And the biggest thanks of all go to my ace editorial team: Wendy Lamb and Dana Carey. It is astonishing how much better my books become under their care.

P.S. I would also like to thank my dog, Sasha, for having all the problems that Cupcake did. Can I write off her vet bills now? Just wondering.

Read more stories of friendship and family by Gennifer Choldenko:

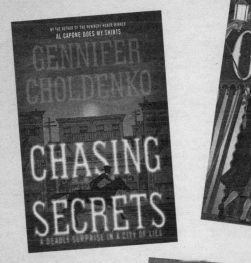